The Chief Legatee by Anna Katharine Green

Anna Katharine Green was born in Brooklyn, New York on November 11th, 1846.

Anna's initial ambition was to be a poet. However that path failed to ignite any significant interest and she turned to fiction writing. She published her first—and most famous work in 1878—'The Leavenworth Case'. Wilkie Collins praised it and it sold extremely well.

It led to Anna writing 40 novels and to becoming known as 'the mother of the detective novel.'

In helping to shape the genre she brought many other innovations including a series detective: her main character was detective Ebenezer Gryce of the New York Metropolitan Police Force, but in three novels he is assisted by the nosy society spinster Amelia Butterworth, another innovation and a prototype for Miss Marple, Miss Silver and others.

She also invented the 'girl detective': in the character of Violet Strange, a debutante with a secret life as a sleuth. Anna's other innovations included the now familiar dead bodies in libraries, newspaper clippings as "clews," the coroner's inquest, and expert witnesses. Yale Law School once used her books to demonstrate how damaging it can be to rely on circumstantial evidence.

Her career was now well advanced and she was much admired.

On November 25, 1884, Green married the actor and stove designer, and later noted furniture maker, Charles Rohlfs, who was seven years her junior. They had three children; Rosamund, Roland and Sterling.

Although Anna was a progressive she did not approve of many of her feminist contemporaries, and was opposed to women's suffrage.

On November 25, 1884, Anna married the actor and noted furniture maker, Charles Rohlfs, who was seven years her junior. They had three children; Rosamund, Roland and Sterling.

Anna Katharine Green died on April 11, 1935 in Buffalo, New York, at the age of 88.

PART I

A WOMAN OF MYSTERY

CHAPTER I

A BRIDE OF FIVE HOURS

"What's up?"

This from the manager of the Hotel — to his chief clerk. "Something wrong in Room 81?"

"Yes, sir. I've just sent for a detective. You were not to be found and the gentleman is desperate. But very anxious to have it all kept quiet; very anxious. I think we can oblige him there, or, at least, we'll try. Am I right, sir?"

"Of course, if—"

"Oh! it's nothing criminal. The lady's missing, that's all; the lady whose name you see here."

The register lay open between them; the clerk's finger, running along the column, rested about half-way down.

The manager bent over the page.

"'Roger J. Ransom and wife,'" he read out in decided astonishment. "Why, they are—"

"You're right. Married to-day in Grace Church. A great wedding; the papers are full of it. Well, she's the lady. They registered here a few minutes before five o'clock and in ten minutes the bride was missing. It's a queer story Mr. Ransom tells. You'd better hear it. Ah, there's our man! Perhaps you'll go up with him."

"You may bet your last dollar on that," muttered the manager. And joining the new-comer, he made a significant gesture which was all that passed between them till they stepped out on the second floor.

"Wanted in Room 81?" the manager now asked.

"Yes, by a man named Ransom."

"Just so. That's the door. Knock—or, rather, I'll knock, for I must hear his story as soon as you do. The reputation of the hotel—"

"Yes, yes, but the gentleman's waiting. Ah! that's better."

The manager had just knocked.

An exclamation from within, a hurried step, and the door fell open. The figure which met their eyes was startling. Distress, anxiety, and an impatience almost verging on frenzy, distorted features naturally amiable if not handsome.

"My wife," fell in a gasp from his writhing lips.

"We have come to help you find her," Mr. Gerridge calmly assured him. Mr. Gerridge was the detective. "Relate the circumstances, sir. Tell us where you were when you first missed her."

Mr. Ransom's glance wandered past him to the door. It was partly open. The manager, whose name was Loomis, hastily closed it. Mr. Ransom showed relief and hurried into his story. It was to this effect:

"I was married to-day in Grace Church. At the altar my bride—you probably know her name, Miss Georgian Hazen—wore a natural look, and was in all respects, so far as any one could see, a happy woman, satisfied with her choice and pleased with the éclat and elegancies of the occasion. Half-way down the aisle this all changed. I remember the instant perfectly. Her hand was on my arm and I felt it suddenly stiffen. I was not alarmed, but I gave her a quick look and saw that something had happened. What, I could not at the moment determine. She didn't answer when I spoke to her and seemed to be mainly concerned in getting out of the church before her emotions overcame her. This she succeeded in doing with my help; and, once in the vestibule, recovered herself so completely, and met all my inquiries with such a gay shrug of the shoulders, that I should have passed the matter over as a mere attack of nerves, if I had not afterwards detected in her face, through all the hurry and excitement of the ensuing reception, a strained expression not at all natural to her. This was still more evident after the congratulations of a certain guest, who, I am sure, whispered to her before he passed on; and when the time came for her to go up-stairs she was so pale and unlike herself that I became seriously alarmed and asked if she felt well enough to start upon the journey we had meditated. Instantly her manner changed. She turned upon me with a look I have been trying ever since to explain to myself, and begged me not to take her out of town to-night but to some quiet hotel where we might rest for a few days before starting on our travels. She looked me squarely in the eye as she made this request and, seeing in her nothing more than a feverish anxiety lest I should make difficulties of some kind, I promised to do what she asked and bade her run away and get herself ready to go and say nothing to any one of our change of plan. She smiled and turned away towards her own room, but presently came hurrying back to ask if I would grant her one more favor. Would I be so good as not to speak to her or expect her to speak to me till we got to the hotel; she was feeling very nervous but was sure that a few minutes of complete rest would entirely restore her; something had occurred (she acknowledged this) which she wanted to think out; wouldn't I grant her this one opportunity of doing so? It was a startling request, but she looked so lovely—pardon me, I must explain my easy acquiescence—that I gave her the assurance she wished and went about my own preparations, somewhat disconcerted but still not at all prepared for what happened afterward. I had absolutely no idea that she meant to leave me."

Mr. Ransom paused, greatly affected; but upon the detective asking him how and when Mrs. Ransom had deserted him, he controlled himself sufficiently to say:

"Here; immediately after that silent and unnatural ride. She entered the office with me and was standing close at my side all the time I was writing our names in the register; but later, when I turned to ask her to enter the elevator with me, she was gone, and the boy who was standing by with our two bags said that she had slipped into the reception-room across the hall. But I didn't find her there or in any of the adjoining rooms. Nor has anybody since succeeded in finding her. She has left the building—left me, and—"

"You want her back again?"

This from the detective, but very dryly.

"Yes. For she was not following her own inclinations in thus abandoning me so soon after the words which made us one were spoken. Some influence was brought to bear on her which she felt unable to resist. I have confidence enough in her to believe that. The rest is mystery—a mystery which I am forced to ask you to untangle. I have neither the necessary calmness nor experience myself."

"But you surely have done something," protested Gerridge. "Telephoned to her late home or—"

"Oh yes, I have done all that, but with no result. She has not returned to her old home. Her uncle has just been here and he is as much mystified by the whole occurrence as I am. He could tell me nothing, absolutely nothing."

"Indeed! and the man, the one who whispered to her during the reception, couldn't you learn anything about him?"

Mr. Ransom's face took on an expression almost ferocious.

"No. He's a stranger to Mr. Fulton; yet Mr. Fulton's niece introduced him to me as a relative."

"A relative? When was that?"

"At the reception. He was introduced as Mr. Hazen (my wife's maiden name, you know), and when I saw how his presence disturbed her, I said to her, 'A cousin of yours?' and she answered with very evident embarrassment, 'A relative';—which you must acknowledge didn't locate him very definitely. Mr. Fulton doesn't know of any such relative. And I don't believe he is a relative. He didn't sit with the rest of the family in the church."

"Ah! you saw him in the church."

"Yes. I noticed him for two reasons. First, because he occupied an end seat and so came directly under my eye in our passage down the aisle. Secondly, because his face of all those which confronted me when I looked for the cause of her sudden agitation, was the only one not turned towards her in curiosity or interest. His eyes were fixed and vacant; his only. That made him conspicuous and when I saw him again I knew him."

"Describe the man."

Mr. Ransom's face lightened up with an expression of strong satisfaction.

"I am going to astonish you," said he. "The fellow is so plain that children must cry at him. He has suffered some injury and his mouth and jaw have such a twist in them that the whole face is thrown out of shape. So you see," continued the unhappy bridegroom, as his eyes flashed from the detective's face to that of the manager's, "that the influence he exerts over my wife is not that of love. No one could love him. The secret's of another kind. What kind, what, what, what? Find out and I'll pay you any amount you ask. She is too dear and of too sensitive a temperament to be subject to a wretch of his appearance. I cannot bear the thought. It stifles, it chokes me; and yet for three hours I've had to endure it. Three hours! and with no prospect of release unless you—"

"Oh, I'll do something," was Gerridge's bland reply. "But first I must have a few more facts. A man such as you describe should be easy to find; easier than the lady. Is he a tall man?"

"Unusually so."

"Dark or light?"

"Dark."

"Any beard?"

"None. That's why the injury to his jaw shows so plainly."

"I see. Is he what you would call a gentleman?"

"Yes, I must acknowledge that. He shows the manners of good society, if he did whisper words into my wife's ear which were not meant for mine."

"And Mr. Fulton knows nothing of him?"

"Nothing."

"Well, we'll drop him for the present. You have a photograph of your wife?"

"Her picture was in all the papers to-night."

"I noticed. But can we go by it? Does it resemble her?"

"Only fairly. She is far prettier. My wife is something uncommon. No picture ever does her justice."

"She looks like a dark beauty. Is her hair black or brown?"

"Black. So black it has purple shades in it."

"And her eyes? Black too?"

"No, gray. A deep gray, which look black owing to her long lashes."

"Very good. Now about her dress. Describe it as minutely as you can. It was a bride's traveling costume, I suppose."

"Yes. That is, I presume so. I know that it was all right and suitable to the occasion, but I don't remember much about it. I was thinking too much of the woman in the gown to notice the gown itself."

"Cannot you tell the color?"

"It was a dark one. I'm sure it was a dark one, but colors are not much in my line. I know she looked well—they can tell you about it at the house. All that I distinctly remember is the veil she had wound so tightly around her face and hat to keep the rice out of her hair that I could not get one glimpse of her features. All nonsense that veil, especially when I had promised not to address her or even to touch her in the cab. And she wore it into the office. If it had not been for that I might have foreseen her intention in time to prevent it."

"Perhaps she knew that."

"It looks as if she did."

"Which means that she was meditating flight from the first."

"From the time she saw that man," Mr. Ransom corrected.

"Just so; from the time she left her uncle's house. Your wife is a woman of means, I believe."

"Yes, unfortunately."

"Why unfortunately?"

"It makes her independent and offers a lure to irresponsible wretches like him."

"Her fortune is large, then?"

"Very large; larger than my own."

Every one knew Mr. Ransom to be a millionaire.

"Left her by her father?"

"No, by some great-uncle, I believe, who made his fortune in the Klondike."

"And entirely under her own control?"

"Entirely so."

"Who is her man of business?"

"Edward Harper, of—Wall Street."

"He's your man. He'll know sooner or later where she is."

"Yes, but later won't do. I must know to-night; or, if that is impossible, to-morrow. Were it not for the mortification it would cause her I should beg you to put on all your force and ransack the city for this bride of five hours. But such publicity is too shocking. I should like to give her a day to reconsider her treatment of me. She cannot mean to leave me for good. She has too much self-respect; to say nothing of her very positive and not to be questioned affection for myself."

The detective looked thoughtful. The problem had its difficulties.

"Are those hers?" he asked at last, pointing to the two trunks he saw standing against the wall.

"Yes. I had them brought up, in the hope that she had slipped away on some foolish errand or other and would yet come back."

"By their heft I judge them to be full; how about her hand-bag?"

"She had only a small bag and an umbrella. They are both here."

"How's that?"

"The colored boy took them at the door. She went away with nothing in her hands."

Gerridge glanced at the bag Mr. Ransom had pointed out, fingered it, then asked the young husband to open it.

He did so. The usual articles and indispensable adjuncts of a nice woman's toilet met their eyes. Also a pocketbook containing considerable money and a case holding more than one valuable jewel.

The eyes of the officer and manager met in ill-disguised alarm.

"She must have been under the most violent excitement to slip away without these," suggested the former. "I'd better be at work. Give me two hours," were his parting words to Mr. Ransom. "By that time I'll either be back or telephone you. You had better stay here; she may return. Though I don't think that likely," he muttered as he passed the manager.

At the door he stopped. "You can't tell me the color of that veil?"

"No."

"Look about the room, sir. There's lots of colors in the furniture and hangings. Don't you see one somewhere that reminds you of her veil or even of her dress?"

The miserable bridegroom looked up from the bag into which he was still staring and, glancing slowly around him, finally pointed at a chair upholstered in brown and impulsively said:

"The veil was like that; I remember now. Brown, isn't it? a dark brown?"

"Yes. And the dress?"

"I can't tell you a thing about the dress. But her gloves—I remember something about them. They were so tight they gaped open at the wrist. Her hands looked quite disfigured. I wondered that so sensible a woman should buy gloves at least two sizes too small for her. I think she was ashamed of them herself, for she tried to hide them after she saw me looking."

"This was in the cab?"

"Yes."

"Where you didn't speak a word?"

"Not a word."

"Though she seemed so very much cut up?"

"No, she didn't seem cut up; only tired."

"How tired?"

"She sat with her head pressed against the side of the cab."

"And a little turned away?"

"Yes."

"As if she shrank from you?"

"A little so."

"Did she brighten when the carriage stopped?"

"She started upright."

"Did you help her out?"

"No, I had promised not to touch her."

"She jumped out after you?"

"Yes."

"And never spoke?"

"Not a word."

Gerridge opened the door, motioned for the manager to follow, and, once in the hall, remarked to that gentleman:

"I should like to see the boy who took her bag and was with them when she slipped away."

CHAPTER II

THE LADY IN NUMBER THREE

The boy was soon found and proved to be more observing in matters of dress than Mr. Ransom. He described with apparent accuracy both the color and cut of the garments worn by the lady who had flitted away so mysteriously. The former was brown, all brown; and the latter was of the tailor-made variety, very natty and becoming. "What you would call 'swell,'" was the comment, "if her walk hadn't spoiled the hang of it. How she did walk! Her shoes must have hurt her most uncommon. I never did see any one hobble so."

"How's that? She hobbled, and her husband didn't notice it?"

"Oh, he had hurried on ahead. She was behind him, and she walked like this."

The pantomime was highly expressive.

"That's a point," muttered Gerridge. Then with a sharp look at the boy: "Where were you that you didn't notice her when she slipped off?"

"Oh, but I did, sir. I was waiting for the clerk to give me the key, when I saw her step back from the gentleman's side and, looking quickly round to see if any one was noticing her, slide off into the reception-room. I thought she wanted a drink of water out of the pitcher on the center-table, but if she did, she didn't come back after she had got it. None of us ever saw her again."

"Did you follow Mr. Ransom when he walked through those rooms?"

"No, sir; I stayed in the hall."

"Did the lady hobble when she slid thus mysteriously out of sight?"

"A little. Not so much as when she came in. But she wasn't at her ease, sir. Her shoes were certainly too small."

"I think I will take a peep at those rooms now," Gerridge remarked to the manager.

Mr. Loomis bowed, and together they crossed the office to the reception-room door. The diagram of this portion of the hotel will give you an idea of these connecting rooms.

There are three of them, as you will see, all reception-rooms. Mr. Ransom had passed through them all in looking for his wife. In No. 1 he found several ladies sitting and standing, all strangers. He encountered no one in No. 2, and in No. 3 just one person, a lady in street costume evidently waiting for some one. To this lady he had addressed himself, asking if she had seen any one pass that way the moment before. Her reply was a decided "No"; that she had been waiting in that same room for several minutes and had seen no one. This staggered him. It was as if his wife had dissolved into thin air. True, she might have eluded him by slipping out into the hall by means of door two at the moment she entered door one; and alert to this possibility, he hastened back into the hall to look for her. But she was nowhere visible, nor had she been observed leaving the building by the man stationed at entrance A. But there was another exit, that of B. Had she gone out that way? Mr. Ransom had taken pains to inquire and had been assured by the man in charge that no lady had left by that door during the last ten minutes. This he had insisted on, and when Mr. Loomis and the detective came in their turn to question him on this point he insisted on it again. The mystery seemed complete,—at least to the manager. But the detective was not quite satisfied. He asked the man if at any time that day, before or after Mrs. Ransom's disappearance, he had swung the door open for a lady who walked lame. The answer was decisive. "Yes; one who walked as if her shoes were tight."

"When?"

"Oh a little while after the gentleman asked his questions."

"Was she dressed in brown?"

That he didn't know. He didn't look at ladies' dresses unless they were something special.

"But she walked lame and she came from Room 3?"

Yes. He remembered that much.

Gerridge, with a nod to the manager, stepped into the open compartment of the whirling door. "I'm off," said he. "Expect to hear from me in two hours."

At twenty minutes to ten Mr. Ransom was called up on the telephone.

"One question, Mr. Ransom."

"Hello, who are you?"

"Gerridge."

"All right, go ahead."

"Did you see the face of the woman you spoke to in Room No. 3?"

"Of course. She was looking directly at me."

"You remember it? Could identify it if you saw it again?"

"Yes; that is—"

"That's all, good-by."

The circuit was cut off.

Another intolerable wait. Then there came a knock on the door and Gerridge entered. He held a photograph in his hand which he had evidently taken from his pocket on his way up.

"Look at this," said he. "Do you recognize the face?"

"The lady—"

"Just so; the one who said she had seen no one come into No. 3 on the first floor."

Mr. Ransom's expression of surprised inquiry was sufficient answer.

"Well, it's a pity you didn't look at her gloves instead of at her face. You might have had some dim idea of having seen them before. It was she who rode to the hotel with you; not your wife. The veil was wound around her face for a far deeper purpose than to ward off rice."

Mr. Ransom staggered back against the table before which he had been standing. The blow was an overwhelming one.

"Who is this woman?" he demanded. "She came from Mr. Fulton's house. More than that, from my wife's room. What is her name and what did she mean by such an outrage?"

"Her name is Bella Burton, and she is your wife's confidential maid. As for the meaning of this outrage, it will take more than two hours to ferret out that. I can only give you the single fact I've mentioned."

"And Mrs. Ransom?"

"She left the house at the same moment you did; you and Miss Burton. Only she went by the basement door."

"She? She?"

"Dressed in her maid's clothes. Oh, you'll have to hear worse things than that before we're out of this muddle. If you won't mind a bit of advice from a man of experience, I would suggest that you take things easy. It's the only way."

Shocked into silence by this cold-blooded philosophy, Mr. Ransom controlled both his anger and his humiliation; but he could not control his surprise.

"What does it mean?" he murmured to himself. "What does it all mean?"

CHAPTER III

"HE KNOWS THE WORD"

The next moment the doubt natural to the occasion asserted itself.

"How do you know all this? You state the impossible. Explain yourself."

Gerridge was only too willing to do so.

"I have just come from Mr. Fulton's house," said he. "Inquiries there elicited the facts which have so startled you. Neither Mr. Fulton nor his wife meant to deceive you. They knew nothing, suspected nothing of what took place, and you have no cause to blame them. It was all a plot between the two women."

"But how—why—"

"You see, I had a fact to go upon. You had noticed that your so-called bride's gloves did not fit her; the boy below, that her shoes were so tight she hobbled. That set me thinking. A woman of Mrs. Ransom's experience and judgment would not be apt to make a mistake in two such important particulars; which, taken with the veil and the promise she exacted from you not to address or touch her during your short ride to the hotel, led me to point my inquiries so that I soon found out that your wife had had the assistance of another woman in getting ready for her journey and that this woman was her own maid who had been with her for a long time, and had always given evidence of an especial attachment for her. Asking about this girl's height and general appearance (for the possibility of a substitution was already in my mind), I found that she was of slight figure and good carriage, and that her age was not far removed from that of her young mistress. This made the substitution I have mentioned feasible, and when I was told that she was seen taking her hat and bonnet into the bride's room, and, though not expected to leave till the next morning, had slid away from the house by the basement door at the same moment her mistress appeared on the front steps, my suspicions became so confirmed that I asked how this girl looked, in the hope that you would be able to recognize her, through the description, as the woman you had seen sitting in Reception-room No. 3. But to my surprise, Mrs. Fulton had what was better than any description, the girl's picture. This has simplified matters very much. By it you have been able to identify the woman who attempted to mislead you in the reception-room, and I the person who rode here with you from Mr. Fulton's house. Wasn't she dressed in brown? Didn't you notice a similarity in her appearance to that of the very lady you were then seeking?"

"I did not observe. Her face was all I saw. She was looking directly at me as I stepped into the room."

"I see. She had taken off her veil and trusted to your attention being caught by her strange features,—as it was. But that dress was brown; I'm sure of it. She was the very woman. Otherwise the mystery is impenetrable. A deep plot, Mr. Ransom; one that should prove to you that Mrs. Ransom's motive in leaving you was of a very serious character. Do you wish that motive probed to the bottom? I cannot do it without publicity. Are you willing to incur that publicity?"

"I must." Mr. Ransom had risen in great excitement. "Nothing can hide the fact that my bride left me on our wedding-day. It only remains now to show that she did it under an influence which robbed her of her own will; an influence from which she shrank even while succumbing to it. I can show her no greater kindness, and I am not afraid of the result. I have perfect confidence in her integrity"—he hesitated, then added with strong conviction—"and in her love."

The detective hid his surprise. He could not understand this confidence. But then he knew nothing of the memories which lay back of it. Not to him could this grievously humiliated and disappointed man reveal the secrets of a courtship which had fixed his heart on this one woman, and aroused in him such trust that even this uncalled-for outrage to his pride and affection had not been able to shake it. Such secrets are sacred; but the reflection of his trust was strong on his face as he repeated:

"Perfect confidence, Mr. Gerridge. Whatever may have drawn Mrs. Ransom from my side, it was not lack of affection, or any doubt of my sincerity or undivided attachment to herself."

The detective may not have been entirely convinced on the first point, but he was discretion itself, and responded quite cheerfully with an emphatic:

"Very well. You still want me to find her. I will do my best, sir; but first, cannot you help me with a suggestion or two?"

"I?"

"There must be some clew to so sudden a freak on the part of a young and beautiful woman, who, I have taken pains to learn, has not only a clean record but a reputation for good sense. The Fultons cannot supply it. She has lived a seemingly open and happy life in their house, and the mystery is as great to them as to you. But you, as her lover and now her husband, must have been favored with confidences not given to others. Cannot you recall one likely to put us on the right track? Some fact prior to the events of to-day, I mean; some fact connected with her past life; before she went to live with the Fultons?"

"No. Yet let me think; let me think." Mr. Ransom dropped his face into his hands and sat for a moment silent. When he looked up again, the detective perceived that the affair was hopeless so far as he was concerned. "No," he repeated, this time with unmistakable emphasis, "she has always appeared buoyant and untrammeled. But then I have only known her six months."

"Tell me her history so far as you know it. What do you know of her life previous to your meeting her?"

"It was a very simple one. She had a country bringing up, having been born in a small village in Connecticut. She was one of three children and the only one who has survived; her sister, who was her twin, died when she was a small child, and a brother some five years ago. Her fortune was willed her, as I have already told you, by a great-uncle. It is entirely in her own hands. Left an orphan early, she lived first with her brother; then when he died, with one relative after another, till lastly she settled down with the Fultons. I know of no secret in her life, no entanglement, not even of any prior engagements. Yet that man with the twisted jaw was not unknown to her, and if he is a relative, as she said, you should have no difficulty in locating him."

"I have a man on his track," Gerridge replied. "And one on the girl's too; I mean, of course, Bela Burton's. They will report here up to twelve o'clock to-night. It is now half-past eleven. We should hear from one or the other soon."

"And my wife?"

"A description of the clothing she wore has gone out. We may hear from it. But I doubt if we do to-night unless she has rejoined her maid or the man with a scar. Somehow I think she will join the girl. But it's hard to tell yet."

Mr. Ransom could hardly control his impatience. "And I must sit helpless here!" he exclaimed. "I who have so much at stake!"

The detective evidently thought the occasion called for whatever comfort it was in his power to bestow.

"Yes," said he. "For it is here she will seek you if she takes a notion to return. But woman is an uncertain quantity," he dryly added.

At that moment the telephone bell rang. Mr. Ransom leaped to answer; but the call was only an anxious one from the Fultons, who wanted to know what news. He answered as best he could, and was recrossing disconsolately to his chair when voices rose in the hall, and a man was ushered in, whom Gerridge immediately introduced as Mr. Sims.

A runner—and with news! Mr. Ransom, summoning up his courage, waited for the inevitable question and reply. They came quickly enough.

"What have you got? Have you found the man?"

"Yes. And the lady's been to see him; that is, if the description of her togs was correct."

"He means Mrs. Ransom," explained Gerridge. Then, as he marked his client's struggle for composure, he quietly asked, "A lady in a dark green suit with yellowish furs and a blue veil over her hat?"

"That's the ticket!"

"The clothes worn by the woman who went out of the basement door, Mr. Ransom."

The latter turned sharply aside. The shame of the thing was becoming intolerable.

"And this woman wearing those yellow furs and the blue veil visited the man of the broken jaw?" inquired Gerridge.

"Yes, sir."

"When?"

"About six this afternoon."

"And where?"

"At the hotel St. Denis where I have since tracked him."

"How long did she stay?"

"About an hour."

"In the parlor or—"

"In the parlor. They had a great deal to say. More than one noticed them, but no one heard anything. They talked very low but they meant business."

"Where is this man now?"

"At the same place. He has engaged a room there."

"The man with the twisted jaw?"

"Yes."

"Under what name?"

"Hugh Porter."

"Ah, it was Hazen only five hours ago," muttered Ransom. "Porter, did you say? I'll have a talk with this Porter at once."

"I think not to-night," put in the detective, with the mingled authority and deference natural to one of his kind. "To-morrow, perhaps, but to-night it would only provoke scandal."

This was certainly true, but Mr. Ransom was not an easy man to dominate.

"I must see him before I sleep," he insisted. "A single word may solve this mystery. He has the word. I'd be a fool to let the night go by—Ah! what's that?"

The telephone bell had rung again. A message from the office this time. A note had just been handed in for Mr. Ransom; should they send it up?

Gerridge was at the 'phone.

"Instantly," he shouted down, "and be sure you hold the messenger. It may be from your lady," he remarked to Mr. Ransom. "Stranger things than that have happened."

Mr. Ransom reeled to the door, opened it and stood waiting. The two detectives exchanged glances. What might not that note contain!

Mr. Ransom opened it in the hall. When he came back into the room, his hand was shaking and his face looked drawn and pale. But he showed no further disposition to go out. Instead, he sank into a chair, with a motion of dismissal to the two detectives.

"Question the boy who brought this," said he. "It is from Mrs. Ransom; written, as you see, at the St. Denis. She bids me farewell for a time, but does not favor me with any explanations. She cannot do differently, she says, and asks me to trust her and wait. Not very encouraging to sleep on; but it's something. She has not entirely forsaken me."

Gerridge with a shrug turned sharply towards the door. "I take it that you wouldn't object to knowing all the messenger can tell you?"

"No, no. Question him. Find out whether she gave this to him with her own hand."

Gerridge obeyed this injunction, but was told in reply that the note had been given him to deliver by a clerk in the hotel lobby. He could tell nothing about the lady.

This was unsatisfactory enough; but the man who had influenced her to this step had been placed under surveillance. To-morrow they would question him; the mystery was not without a promise of solution. So Gerridge felt; but not Mr. Ransom; for at the end of the lines whose purport he had just communicated to the detective were these few, significant words:

"Make no move to find me. If you love me well enough to wait in silence for developments, happiness may yet be ours."

CHAPTER IV

MR. RANSOM WAITS

Gerridge rose early, primed, as he said to himself, for business. But to his great disappointment he found Mr. Ransom in a frame of mind which precluded action. Indeed, that gentleman looked greatly changed. He not only gave evidence of a sleepless night but showed none of the spirit of the previous evening, and hesitated quite painfully when Gerridge asked him if he did not intend to go ahead with the interview they had promised themselves.

"That's as it may be," was the hesitating reply. "I hardly think that I shall visit the man you mean this morning. He interests me and I hope that none of his movements will escape you. But I'm not ready to talk to him. I prefer to wait a little; to give my wife a chance. I should feel better, and have less to forget."

"Just as you say," returned the detective stiffly. "He's under our thumb at present, I can't tell when he may wriggle out."

"Not while your eye's on him. And your eye won't leave him as long as you have confidence in the reward I've promised you."

"Perhaps not; but you take the life out of me. Last night you were too hot; this morning you are too cold. But it's not for me to complain. You know where to find me when you want me." And without more ado the detective went out.

Mr. Ransom remained alone and in no enviable frame of mind. He was distrustful of himself, distrustful of the man who had made all this trouble, and distrustful of her, though he would not acknowledge it. Every baser instinct in him drove him to the meeting he declined. To see the man—to force from him the truth, seemed the only rational thing to do. But the final words of his wife's letter stood in his way. She had advised patience. If patience would clear the situation and bring him the result he so ardently desired, then he would be patient—that is, for a day; he did not promise to wait longer. Yes, he would give her a day. That was time enough for a man suffering on the rack of such an intolerable suspense— one day.

But even that day did not pass without breaks in his mood and more than one walk in the direction of the St. Denis Hotel. If Gerridge's eye was on him as well as on the special object of his surveillance, he must have smiled, more than once, at the restless flittings of his client about the forbidden spot. In the evening it was the same, but the next morning he remained steadfastly at his hotel. He had laid out his future course in these words: "I will extend the time to three days; then if I do not hear from her I will get that wry-necked fellow by the throat and twist an explanation from him." But the three days passed and he found the situation unchanged. Then he set as his limit the end of the week, but before the full time had elapsed he was advised by Gerridge that he himself was being followed in his turn by a couple of private detectives; and while still under the agitation of this discovery was further disconcerted by having the following communication thrust into his hand in the open street by a young woman who succeeded in losing herself in the crowd before he had got so much as a good look at her.

You can judge of his amazement as he read the few lines it contained.

Read the papers to-night and forget the stranger at the St. Denis.

That was all. But the writing was hers. The hours passed slowly till the papers were cried in the street. What Mr. Ransom read in them increased his astonishment, I might say his anxiety. It was a paragraph about his wife, an almost incredible one, running thus:

A strange explanation is given of the disappearance of Mrs. Roger Ransom on her wedding-day. As our readers will remember, she accompanied her husband to the hotel, but managed to slip away and leave the house while he still stood at the desk. This act, for which nothing in her previous conduct has in any way prepared her friends, is now said to have been due to the shock of hearing, some time during her wedding-day, that a sister whom she had supposed dead was really alive and in circumstances of almost degrading poverty. As this sister had been her own twin the effect upon her mind was very serious. To find and rescue this sister she left her newly made husband in the surreptitious manner already recorded in the papers. That she is not fully herself is shown by her continued secrecy as to her whereabouts. All that she has been willing to admit to the two persons she has so far taken into her confidence—her husband and the agent who conducts her affairs—is that she has found her sister and cannot leave her. Why, she does not state. The case is certainly a curious one and Mr. Ransom has the sympathy of all his friends.

Confused, and in a state of mind bordering on frenzy, Mr. Ransom returned to the hotel and sought refuge in his own room. He put no confidence in what he had just read; he regarded it as a newspaper story and a great fake; but she had bid him read it, and this fact in itself was very disturbing. For how could she have known about it if she had not been its author, and if she was its author, what purpose had she expected it to serve?

He was still debating this question when he reached his own room. On the floor, a little way from the sill, lay a letter. It had been thrust under the door during his absence. Lifting it in some trepidation, he cast a glance at its inscription and sank staggering into the nearest chair, asking himself if he had the courage to open and read it. For the handwriting, like that of the note handed him in the street, was Georgian's, and he felt himself in a maze concerning her which made everything in her connection seem dreamlike and unreal. It was not long, however, before he had mastered its contents. They were strange enough, as this transcription of them will show.

You have seen what has happened to me, but you cannot understand how I feel. She looks exactly like me. It is that which makes the world eddy about me. I cannot get used to it. It is like seeing my own reflected image step from the mirror and walk about doing things. Two of us, Roger, two! If you saw her you would call her Georgian. And she says that she knows you, admires you! and she says it in my voice! I try to shut my ears, but I hear her saying it even when her lips do not move. She is as ignorant as she is afflicted and I cannot leave her. She cannot hear a sound, though she can talk well enough about what is going on in her own mind, and she is so wayward and uncertain of temper, owing to her ignorance and her difficulty in understanding me, that I don't know what she would do if once let out of my sight. I love you—I love you—but I must stay right here.

Your affectionate and most unhappy

Georgian.

The sheet with its tear-stained lines fell from his grasp. Then he caught it up again and looked carefully at the signature. It was his wife's without doubt. Then he studied the rest of the writing and compared it with that of the note which had been thrust into his hands earlier in the day. There was no difference between them except that there were evidences of faltering in the latter, not noticeable in the earlier communication. As he noted these tokens of weakness or suffering, he caught up the telephone receiver in good earnest and called out Gerridge's number. When the detective answered, he shouted back:

"Have you read the evening papers? If you haven't, do so at once; then come directly to me. It's business now and no mistake; and our first visit shall be on the fellow at the St. Denis."

CHAPTER V

IN CORRIDOR AND IN ROOM

Three quarters of an hour later Mr. Ransom and Gerridge stood in close conference before the last mentioned hotel. The former was peremptory in what he had to say.

"I haven't a particle of confidence in this newspaper story," he declared. "I haven't much confidence in her letter. It is this man who is working us. He has a hold on her and has given her this cock and bull story to tell. A sister! A twin sister come to light after fifteen years of supposed burial! I find the circumstance entirely too romantic. Nor does an explanation of this nature fit the conditions. She was happy before she saw him in the church. He isn't her twin sister. I tell you the game is a deep one and she is the sufferer. Her letters betray more than a disturbed mind; they betray a disturbed brain. That man is the cause and I mean to wring his secret from him. You are sure of his being still in the house?"

"He was early this morning. He has lived a very quiet life these last few days, the life of one waiting. He has not even had visitors, after that one interview he held with your wife. I have kept careful watch on him. Though a suspected character, he has done nothing suspicious while I've had him under my eye."

"That's all right and I thank you, Gerridge; but it doesn't shake my opinion as to his being the moving power in this fraud. For fraud it is and no mistake. Of that I am fully convinced. Shall we go up? I want to surprise him in his own room where he cannot slip away or back out."

"Leave that business to me; I'll manage it. If you want to see him in his room, you shall."

But this time the detective counted without his host. Mr. Porter was not in his room but in one of the halls. They encountered him as they left the elevator. He was standing reading a newspaper. The disfigured jaw could not be mistaken. They stopped where they were and looked at him.

He was intent, absorbed. As they watched, they saw his hands close convulsively on the sheet he was holding, while his lips muttered some words that made the detective look hard at his companion.

"Did you hear?" he cautiously inquired, as Mr. Ransom stood hesitating, not knowing whether to address the man or not.

"No; what did he say? Do you suppose he is reading that paragraph?"

"I haven't a doubt of it; and his words were, 'Here's a damned lie!'—very much like your own, sir."

Mr. Ransom drew the detective a few steps down the corridor.

"He said that?"

"Yes, I heard him distinctly."

"Then my theory is all wrong. This man didn't provide her with this imaginary twin sister."

"Evidently not."

"And is as surprised as we are."

"And about as much put out. Look at him! Nothing yellow there! We shall have to go easy with him."

Mr. Ransom looked and felt a recoil of more than ordinary dislike for the man. The latter had put the paper in his pocket and was coming their way. His face, once possibly handsome, for his eyes and forehead were conspicuously fine, showed a distortion quite apart from that given by his physical disfigurement. He was not simply angry but in a mental and moral rage, and it made him more than hideous; it made him appalling. Yet he said nothing and moved along very quietly, making, to all appearance, for his room. Would he notice them as he went by? It did not seem likely. Instinctively they had stepped to one side, and Mr. Ransom's face was in the shadow. To both it had seemed better not to accost him while he was in this mood. They would see him later.

But this was not to be. Some instinct made him turn, and Mr. Ransom, recognizing his opportunity, stepped forward and addressed him by the name under which he had introduced himself at the reception; that of his wife's family, Hazen.

The effect was startling. Instead of increasing his anger, as the detective had naturally expected, it appeared to have the contrary effect, for every vestige of passion immediately disappeared from his face, leaving only its natural disfigurement to plead against him. He approached them, and Ransom, at least, was conscious of a revulsion of feeling in his favor, there was such restraint and yet such undoubted power in his strange and peculiar personality.

"You know me?" said he, darting a keen and comprehensive look from one to the other.

"We should like a few words with you," ventured Gerridge. "This gentleman thinks you can give him very valuable information about a person he is greatly interested in."

"He is mistaken." The words came quick and decisive in a not unmelodious voice. "I am a stranger in New York; a stranger in this country. I have few, if any, acquaintances."

"You have one."

It was now Mr. Ransom's turn.

"A man with no acquaintances does not attend weddings; certainly not wedding receptions. I have seen you at one, my own. Do you not recognize me, Mr. Hazen?"

A twitch of surprise, not even Ransom could call it alarm, drew his mouth still further towards his ear; but his manner hardly altered and it was in the same affable tone that he replied:

"You must pardon my short-sightedness. I did not recognize you, Mr. Ransom."

"Did not want to," muttered Gerridge, satisfied in his own mind that this man was only deterred by his marked and unmistakable physiognomy from denying the acquaintanceship just advanced.

"Your congratulations did not produce the desired effect," continued Mr. Ransom. "My happiness was short lived. Perhaps you knew its uncertain tenure when you wished me joy. I remember that your tone lacked sincerity."

It was a direct attack. Whether a wise one or not remained to be seen. Gerridge watched the unfolding drama with interest.

"I have reason to think," proceeded Mr. Ransom, "that the unhappy termination of that day's felicities were in a measure due to you. You seem to know my bride very well; much too well for her happiness or mine."

"We will argue that question in my room," was the unmoved reply. "The open hall is quite unsuited to a conversation of this nature. Now," said he, turning upon them when they were in the privacy of his small but not uncomfortable apartment, "you will be kind enough to repeat what you just said. I wish to thoroughly understand you."

"You have the right," returned Mr. Ransom, controlling himself under the detective's eye. "I said that your presence at this wedding seemed to disturb my wife, which fact, considering the after occurrences of the day, strikes me as important enough for discussion. Are you willing to discuss it affably and fairly?"

"May I ask who your companion is?" inquired the other, with a slight inclination towards Gerridge.

"A friend; one who is in my confidence."

"Then I will answer you without any further hesitation. My presence may have disturbed your wife, it very likely did, but I was not to blame for that. No man is to blame for the bad effects of an unfortunate accident."

"Oh, I don't mean that," Mr. Ransom hastened to protest. "The cause of her very evident agitation was not personal. It had a deeper root than that. It led, or so I believe, to her flight from a love she cherished, at a moment when our mutual life seemed about to begin."

The impassive, I might almost say set features of this man of violent passions but remarkable self-restraint failed to relax or give any token of the feelings with which he listened to this attack.

"Then the news given of your wife in the papers to-night is false," was his quiet retort. "It professes to give a distinct, if somewhat fantastic, reason for her flight. A reason totally different from the one you suggest."

"A reason you don't believe in?"

"Certainly not. It is too bizarre."

"I share your incredulity. That is why I seek the truth from you rather than from the columns of a newspaper. And you owe me this truth. You have broken up my life."

"I? That's a strange accusation you make, Mr. Ransom."

"Possibly. But it's one which strikes hard on your conscience, for all that. This is evident enough even to a stranger like myself. I am convinced that if you had not come into her life she would have been at my side to-day. Now, who are you? She told me you were a relative."

"She told you the truth; I am. Her nearest relative. The story in the paper has a certain amount of truth in it. Her brother, not her sister, has come back from the grave. I am that brother. She was once devoted to me."

"You are—"

"Yes. Oh, there'll be no difficulty in my proving this relationship. I have evidence upon evidence of the fact right in this room with me; evidence much more convincing and far less disputable than this surprising twin can bring forward if her identity is questioned. Georgian had a twin sister, but she was buried years ago. I was never buried. I simply did not return from a well-known and dangerous voyage. The struggle I had for life—you cannot want the details now—has left its indelible impress in the scar which has turned me from a personable man into what some people might call a monstrosity. And it is this scar which has kept me so long from home and country. It has taken me four years to make up my mind to face again my family and friends. And now that I have, I find that it would have been better for us all if I had stayed away. Georgian saw me and her mind wavered. In no other way can I account for her wild behavior since that hour. That is all I have to say, sir. I think I am almost as much an object of pity as yourself."

And for a moment he appeared to be so, not only to Gerridge, but to Mr. Ransom himself. Then something in the man—his unnatural coldness, the purpose which made itself felt through all his self-restraint—reawakened Mr. Ransom's distrust and led him to say:

"Your complaint is natural. If you are Mrs. Ransom's brother, there should be sympathy between us and not antagonism. But I feel only antagonism. Why is this?"

A shrug, followed by an odd smile.

"You should be able to account for that on very reasonable grounds," said he. "I do not expect much mercy from strangers. It is hard to make your good intentions felt through such a distorted medium as my expression has now become."

"Mrs. Ransom has been here," Ransom suddenly launched forth. "Within two hours of your encounter under Mr. Fulton's roof, she was talking with you in this hotel. I have proof positive of that, sir."

"I have no wish to deny the fact," was the steady answer. "She did come here and we had a talk; it was necessary; I wanted money."

The last phrase was uttered with such grim determination that the exclamation which had risen to Mr. Ransom's lips died in a conflict of feeling which forbade any rejoinder that savored of sarcasm. Hazen, however, must have noted his first look, for he added with an air of haughty apology:

"I repeat that we were once very fond of each other."

Ransom felt his perplexities growing with every moment he talked with this man. He remembered the money which both he and Gerridge had seen in her bag,—an amount too large for her to have retained very much on her person,—and following the instinct of the moment, he remarked:

"Mrs. Ransom is not the woman to hesitate when a person she loves makes an appeal for money. She handed you immediately a large sum, I have no doubt."

"She wrote me out a check," was the simple but cold answer.

Mr. Ransom felt the failure of his attempt and stole a glance at Gerridge.

The doubtful smile he received was not very encouraging. The same thought had evidently struck both. The money in the bag was a blind—she had carried her check-book with her and so could draw on her account for whatever she wished. But under what name? Her maiden one or his? Ransom determined to find out.

"I do not begrudge you the money," said he, "but Mrs. Ransom's signature had changed a few hours previous to her making out this check. Did she remember this?"

"She signed her married name promising to notify the bank at once."

"And you cashed the check?"

"No, sir; I am not in such immediate need of money as that. I have it still, but I shall endeavor to cash it to-morrow. Some question may come up as to her sanity, and I do not choose to lose the only money she has ever been in a position to give me."

"Mr. Hazen, you harp on the irresponsible condition of her mind. Did you see any tokens of this in the interview you had together?"

"No; she seemed sane enough then; a little shocked and troubled, but quite sane."

"You knew that she had stolen away from me—that she had resorted to a most unworthy subterfuge in order to hold this conversation with you?"

"No; I had asked her to come, and on that very afternoon if possible, but I never knew what means she took for doing so; I didn't ask and she didn't say."

"But she talked of her marriage? She must have said something about an event which is usually considered the greatest in a woman's life."

"Yes, she spoke of it."

"And of me?"

"Yes, she spoke of you."

"And in what terms? I cannot refrain from asking you, Mr. Hazen, I am in such ignorance as to her real attitude towards me; her conduct is so mysterious; the reasons she gives for it so puerile."

"She said nothing against you or her marriage. She mentioned both, but not in a manner that would add to your or my knowledge of her intentions. My sister disappointed me, sir. She was much less open than I wished. All that I could make out of her manner and conversation was the overpowering shock she felt at seeing me again and seeing me so changed. She didn't even tell me when and where we might meet again. When she left, she was as much lost to me as she was to you, and I am no less interested in finding her than you are yourself. I had no idea she did not mean to return to you when she went away from this hotel."

Mr. Ransom sprang upright in an agitation the other may have shared, but of which he gave no token.

"Do you mean to say," he asked, "that you cannot tell me where the woman you call your sister is now?"

"No more than you can give me the same necessary information in regard to your wife. I am waiting like yourself to hear from her—and waiting with as little hope."

Had he seen Ransom's hand close convulsively over the pocket in which her few strange words to him were lying, that a slight tinge of sarcasm gave edge to the last four words?

"But this is not like my wife," protested Ransom, hesitating to accuse the other of falsehood, yet evidently doubting him from the bottom of his heart. "Why deceive us both? She was never a disingenuous woman."

"In childhood she had her incomprehensible moments," observed Hazen, with an ambiguous lift of his shoulders; then, as Ransom made an impatient move, added with steady composure: "I have candidly answered all your questions whether agreeable or otherwise, and the fact that I am as much shocked as yourself by these mad and totally incredible statements of hers about a newly recovered sister should prove to you that she is not following any lead of mine in this dissemination of a bare-faced falsehood."

There was truth in this which both Mr. Ransom and Gerridge felt obliged to own. Yet they were not satisfied, even after Mr. Hazen, almost against Mr. Ransom's will, had established his claims to the relationship he professed, by various well-attested documents he had at hand. Instinct could not be juggled with, nor could Ransom help feeling that the mystery in which he found himself entangled had been deepened rather than dispelled by the confidences of this new brother-in-law.

"The maze is at its thickest," he remarked as he left a few minutes later with the perplexed Gerridge. "How shall I settle this new question? By what means and through whose aid can I gain an interview with my wife?"

CHAPTER VI

The answer was an unexpectedly sensible one.

"Hunt up her man of business and see what he can do for you. She cannot get along without money; nor could that statement of hers have got into the papers without somebody's assistance. Since she did not get it from the fellow we have just left, she must have had it from the only other person she would dare confide in."

Ransom answered by immediately hailing a down-town car.

The interview which followed was certainly a remarkable one. At first Mr. Harper would say nothing, declaring that his relations with Mrs. Ransom were of a purely business and confidential nature. But by degrees, moved by the persuasive influence of Mr. Ransom's candor and his indubitable right to consideration, he allowed himself to admit that he had seen Mrs. Ransom during the last three days and that he had every reason to believe that there was a twin sister in the case and that all Mrs. Ransom's eccentric conduct was attributable to this fact and the overpowering sense of responsibility which it seemed to have brought to her—a result which would not appear strange to those who knew the sensitiveness of her nature and the delicate balance of her mind.

Mr. Ransom recalled the tenor of her strange letter on this subject, but was not convinced. He inquired of Mr. Harper if he had heard her say anything about the equally astounding fact of a returned brother, and when he found that this was mere jargon to Mr. Harper, he related what he knew of Hazen and left the lawyer to draw his own inferences.

The result was some show of embarrassment on the part of Mr. Harper. It was evident that in her consultations with him she had entirely left out all allusion to this brother. Either the man had advanced a false claim or else she was in an irresponsible condition of mind which made her see a sister where there was a brother.

Ransom made some remark indicative of his appreciation of the dilemma in which they found themselves, but was quickly silenced by the other's emphatic assertion:

"I have seen the girl; she was with Mrs. Ransom the day she came here. She sat in the adjoining room while we talked over her case in this one."

"You saw her—saw her face?"

"No, not her face; she was too heavily veiled for that. Mrs. Ransom explained why. They were too absurdly alike, she said. It awoke comment and it gave her the creeps. But their figures were identical though their dresses were different."

"So! there is some one then; the girl is not absolutely a myth."

"Far from it. Nor is the will which Mrs. Ransom has asked me to draw up for her a myth."

"Her will! she has asked you to draw up her will!"

"Yes. That was the object of her visit. She had entered the married state, she said, and wished to make a legal disposition of her property before she returned to you. She was very nervous when she said this; very nervous through all the interview. There was nothing else for me to do but comply."

"And you have drawn up this will?"

"According to her instructions, yes."

"But she has not signed it?"

"Not yet."

"But she intends to?"

"Certainly."

"Then you will see her again?"

"Naturally."

"Is the time set?"

The lawyer rose to his feet. He understood the hint implied and for an instant appeared to waver. There was something very winsome about Roger Ransom; some attribute or expression which appealed especially to men.

"I wish I might help you out of your difficulty," said he. "But a client's wishes are paramount. Mrs. Ransom desired secrecy. She had every right to demand it of me."

Mr. Ransom's face fell. Hope had flashed upon him only to disappear again. The lawyer eyed him out of the corner of his eye, his mouth working slightly as he walked to and fro between his desk and the door.

"Mrs. Ransom will not always feel herself hampered by a sister, or, if you prefer it, a brother who has so inconveniently come back from the dead. You will have the pleasure of her society some day. There is no doubt about her affection for you."

"But that isn't it," exclaimed the now thoroughly discouraged husband. "I am afraid for her reason, afraid for her life. There is something decidedly wrong somewhere. Don't you see that I must have an immediate interview with her if only to satisfy myself that she aggravates her own danger? Why should she make a will in this underhanded way? Does she fear opposition from me? I have a fortune equal to her own. It is something else she dreads. What? I feel that I ought to know if only to protect her against herself. I would even promise not to show myself or to speak."

"I am sorry to have to say good afternoon, Mr. Ransom. Have you any commands that I can execute for you?"

"None but to give her my love. Tell her there is not a more unhappy man in New York; you may add that I trust her affection."

The lawyer bowed. Mr. Ransom and Gerridge withdrew. At the foot of the stairs they were stopped by the shout of a small boy behind them.

"Say, mister, did you drop something?" he called down, coming meanwhile as rapidly after them as the steepness of the flight allowed. "Mr. Harper says, he found this where you gentlemen were sitting."

Mr. Ransom, somewhat startled, took the small paper offered him. It was none of his property but he held to it just the same. In the middle of a torn bit of paper he had read these words written in his own wife's hand:

Hunter's Tavern,
Sitford, Connecticut.
At 9 o'clock April the 15th.

"By Jove!" he exclaimed, "no one will ever hear me say again that lawyers are devoid of heart?"

CHAPTER VII

RAIN

Mr. Ransom had never heard of Sitford, but upon inquiry learned that it was a small manufacturing town some ten miles from the direct route of travel, to which it was only connected by a stage-coach running once a day, late in the afternoon.

What a spot for a meeting of this kind! Why chosen by her? Why submitted to by this busy New York lawyer? Was this another mystery; or had he misinterpreted Mr. Harper's purpose in passing over to him the address of this small town? He preferred to think the former. He could hardly contemplate now the prospect of failing to see her again which must follow any mistake as to this being the place agreed upon for the signing of her will.

Meantime he had said nothing to Gerridge. This was a hope too personal to confide in a man of his position. He would go to Sitford and endeavor to catch a glimpse of his wife there. If successful, the whole temper of his mind might change towards the situation, if not toward her. He would at least have the satisfaction of seeing her. The detective had enough to do in New York.

April the fifteenth fell on Tuesday. He was not minded to wait so long but took the boat on Monday afternoon. This landed him some time before daylight at the time-worn village from which the coach ran to Sitford. A railway connected this village with New York, necessitating no worse inconvenience than crossing the river on a squat, old-fashioned ferry boat; but he calculated that both the lawyer and Mrs. Ransom would make use of this, and felt the risk would be less for him if he chose the slower and less convenient route.

He had given his name on the boat as Roger Johnston, which was true so far as it went, and he signed this same name at the hotel where he put up till morning. The place was an entirely unknown one to him and he was unknown to it. Both fortuitous facts, he thought, in the light of his own perplexity as to the position in which he really stood towards this mysterious wife of his.

The coach, as I have said, ran late in the afternoon. This was to accommodate the passengers who came by rail. But Mr. Ransom had not planned to go by coach. That would be to risk a premature encounter with his wife, or at least with the lawyer. He preferred to hire a team, and be driven there by some indifferent livery-stable man. Neither prospect was pleasing. It had been raining all night, and bade fair to rain all day. The river was clouded with mist; the hills, which are the glory of the place, were obliterated from the landscape, and the road—he had never seen such a road, all little pools and mud.

However, there was no help for it. The journey must be made, and seeing a livery-stable sign across the road, lost no time in securing the conveyance he needed. At nine o'clock he started out.

The rain drove so fiercely from the northwest,—the very direction in which they were traveling,—that enjoyment of the scenery was impossible. Nor could any pleasure be got out of conversation with the man who drove him. Rain, rain, that was all; and the splash of mud over the wheels which turned all too slowly for his comfort. And there were to be ten miles of this. Naturally he turned to his thoughts and they were all of her.

Why had he not known her better before linking his fate to hers? Why had he never encouraged her to talk to him more about herself and her early life? Had he but done so, he might now have some clew to the mystery devouring him. He might know why so rich and independent a woman had chosen this remote town on an inaccessible road, for the completion of an act which was in itself a mystery. Why could not the will have been signed in New York? But he was not inquisitive in those days. He had taken her for what she seemed—an untrammeled, gay-hearted girl, ready to love and be his happy wife and lifelong companion; and he had been contented to keep all conversation along natural lines and do no probing. And now,—this brother whom all had thought dead, come to life with menace in his acts and conversation! Also a sister,—but this sister he had no belief in. The coincidence was too startlingly out of nature for him to accept a brother and a sister too. A brother or a sister; but not both. Not even Mr. Harper's assurances should influence his credulity to this extent. "Money! money is at the bottom of it all," was his final decision. "She knows it and is making her will, as a possible protection. But why come here?"

Thus every reflection ended.

Suddenly a vanished, half-forgotten memory came back. It brought a gleam of light into the darkness which had hitherto enveloped the whole matter. She had once spoken to him of her early life. She had mentioned a place where she used to play as a child; had mentioned it lovingly, longingly. There were hills, she had said; hills all around. And woods full of chestnut-trees, safe woods where she could wander at will. And the roads—how she loved to walk the roads. No automobiles then, not even bicycles. One could go miles without meeting man or horse. Sometimes a heavily-laden cart would go by drawn by a long string of oxen; but they were picturesque and added to the charm. Oxen were necessary where there was no railroad.

As he repeated these words to himself, he looked up. Through the downpour his eyes could catch a glimpse of the road before him, winding up a long hillside. Down this road was approaching a dozen yoke of oxen dragging a wagon piled with bales of some sort of merchandise. One question in his mind was answered. This spot was not an unknown one to her. It was connected with her childhood days. There was reason back of her choice of it as a place of meeting between her and her lawyer, or if not reason, association, and that of the tenderest kind. He felt himself relieved of the extreme weight of his oppression and ventured upon asking a question or two about Sitford, which he took pains to say he was visiting for the first time.

The information he obtained was but meager, but he did learn that there was a very fair tavern there and that the manufactures of the place were sufficient to account for a stranger's visit. The articles made were mostly novelties.

This knowledge he meant to turn to account, but changed his mind when they finally splashed into town and stopped before the tavern which had been so highly recommended by his driver. The house, dripping though it was from every eave, had such a romantic air that he thought he could venture to cite other reasons for his stay there than the prosaic one of business. That is, if the landlady should give any evidence of being at all in accord with her quaint home and picturesque surroundings.

She showed herself and he at once gave her credit for being all he could wish in the way of credulity and good-nature, and meeting her with the smile which had done good execution in its day, he asked if she had a room for a writer who was finishing a book, and who only asked for quiet and regular meals before his own cosy fire. This to rouse her imagination and make her amenable to his wishes for secrecy.

She was a simple soul and fell easily into the trap. In half an hour Mr. Ransom was ensconced in a pleasant room over the porch, a room which he soon learned possessed many advantages. For it not only overlooked the main entrance, but was so placed as to command a view of all the rooms on his hall. In two of those rooms he bade fair to be greatly interested, Mrs. Deo having remarked that they were being prepared for a lady who was coming that night. As he had no doubt who this lady was, he encouraged the good woman to talk, and presently had the satisfaction of hearing her say that she was very happy over this lady's coming, as she was a Sitford girl, one of the old family of Hazens, and though married now and very rich was much loved by every one in town because she had never forgotten Sitford or Sitford people.

She was coming! He had made no mistake. And this was the place of her birth, just as he had decided when he saw that long line of oxen! He realized how fortunate he was, or rather how indebted he was to Mr. Harper, since in this place only could he hope to gain satisfaction on the mooted point raised by that same gentleman. If she had been born here, so had her twin sister; so had the brother whose claims lay counter to that sister's. Both must have been known to these people, their persons, their history and the circumstances of their supposed deaths. The clews thus afforded must prove invaluable to him. From them he must soon be able to ascertain in which story to place faith and which claimant to believe. He might have interrogated his hostess, but feared to show his interest in the supposed stranger. He preferred to wait a few hours and gather his facts from other lips.

Meantime it rained.

CHAPTER VIII

ELIMINATION

At about three o'clock in the afternoon Mr. Ransom left his room. He had been careful almost from his first arrival to sit with his door ajar. He had, therefore, only to give it a slight push and walk out when he heard the bustle of preparation going on in the two rooms in whose future occupancy he was so vitally interested. A maid stood in the hall. A man within was pushing about furniture. The landlady was giving orders. His course down-stairs did not lead him so far as those rooms, so he called out pleasantly:

"I have written till my head aches, Mrs. Deo. I must venture out notwithstanding the rain. In which direction shall I find the best walking?"

She came to him all eagerness and smiles. "It's all bad, such a day," said she, "but it's muddiest down by the factories. You had better climb the hill."

"Where the cemetery is?" he asked.

"Yes; do you object to cemeteries? Ours is thought to be very interesting. We have stones there whose inscriptions are a hundred and fifty years old. But it's a bad day to walk amongst graves. Perhaps you had better go east. I'm sorry we should have such a storm on your first day. Must you go out?"

He forced a suffering look into his eyes, and insisting that nothing but outdoor air would help him when he had a headache, hastened down-stairs and so out. A blinding gust seized him as he faced the hill, but he drew down his umbrella and hurried on. He had a purpose in following her suggestion as to a walk in this direction. Dark as the grasses were, he meant to search the cemetery for the graves of the Hazens and see what he could learn from them.

He met three persons on his way, all of whom turned to look at him. This was in the village. On the hillside he met nobody. Wind and rain and mud were all; desolation in the prospect and all but desolation in his heart. At the brow he first caught sight of the broken stone wall which separated the old burying place from the road. There lay his path. Happily he could tread it unnoticed and unwatched. There was no one within sight, high or low.

He spent a half hour among the tombs before he struck the name he was looking for. Another ten minutes before he found those of his wife's family. Then he had his reward. On a low brown shaft he read the names of father and mother, and beneath them the following lines:

Sacred to the memory of
Anitra
Died June 7, 1885
Aged 6 years and one day.
Of such is the Kingdom of heaven.

The twin! Georgian was mad. This record showed that her little sister lay here. Anitra,—yes, that was the name of her other half. He remembered it well. Georgian had mentioned it to him more than once. And this child, this Anitra, had been buried here for fifteen years.

Deeply indignant at his wife's duplicity, he took a look at the opposite side of the shaft where still another surprise awaited him. Here was the record of the brother; the brother he had so lately talked to and who had seemingly proven his claim to the name he now read:

Alfred Francesco, only son of Georgian Toritti afterwards Georgian Hazen.
Lost at sea February, 1895.
Aged twenty-five years.

An odd inscription opening up conjectures of the most curious and interesting nature. But it was not this fact which struck him at the time, it was the possibility underlying the simple statement, Lost at sea. This, as the wry-necked man had said, admitted of a possible resurrection. Here was no body. A mound showed where Anitra had been laid away; a little mound surmounted by a headstone carved with her name. But only these few words gave evidence of the young man's death, and inscriptions of this nature are sometimes false.

The conclusion was obvious. It was the brother and not the sister who had reappeared. Georgian was not only playing him false but deceiving the general public. In fact, knowingly or unknowingly, she was perpetrating a great fraud. He was inclined to think unknowingly. He began to regard with less incredulity Hazen's declaration that the shock of her brother's return had unsettled her mind.

Distressed, but no longer the prey of distracting doubt, he again examined the inscription before him and this time noticed its peculiarities. Alfred Francesco, only son of Georgian Toritti afterwards Georgian Hazen. Afterwards! What was meant by that afterwards? That the woman had been married twice, and that this Alfred Francesco was the son of her first husband rather than of the one whose name he bore? It looked that way. There was a suggestion of Italian parentage in the Francesco which corresponded well with the decidedly Italian Toritti.

Perplexed and not altogether satisfied with his discoveries, he turned to leave the place when he found himself in the presence of a man carrying a kit of tools and wearing on his face a harsh and discontented expression. As this man was middle-aged and had no other protection from the rain than a rubber cape for his shoulders, the cause of his discontent was easy enough to imagine; though why he should come into this place with tools was more than Mr. Ransom could understand.

"Hello, stranger." It was this man who spoke. "Interested in the Hazen monument, eh? Well, I'll soon give you reason to be more interested yet. Do you see this inscription—On June 7, 1885; Anitra, aged six, and the rest of it? Well, I cut them letters there fifteen years ago. Now I'm to cut 'em out. The orders has just come. The youngster didn't die it seems, and I'm commanded to chip the fifteen-year-old lie out. What do you think of that? A sweet job for a day like this. Mor'n likely it'll put me under a stone myself. But folks won't listen to reason. It's been here fifteen years and seventeen days and now it must come out, rain or shine, before night-fall. 'Before the sun sets,' so the telegram ran. I'll be blessed but I'll ask a handsome penny for this job."

Mr. Ransom, controlling himself with difficulty, pointed to the little mound. "But the child seems to have been buried here," he said.

"Lord bless you, yes, a child was buried here, but we all knew years ago that it mightn't be Hazen's. The schoolhouse burned and a dozen children with it. One of the little bodies was given to Mr. Hazen for burial. He believed it was his Anitra, but a good while after, a bit of the dress she wore that day was found hanging to a bush where some gipsies had been. There were lots of folks who remembered that them gipsies had passed the schoolhouse a half hour before the fire, and they now say found the little girl hiding behind the wood-pile, and carried her off. No one ever knew; but her death was always thought doubtful by every one but Mr. and Mrs. Hazen. They stuck to the old idee and believed her to be buried under this mound where her name is."

"But one of the children was buried here," persisted Ransom. "You must have known the number of those lost and would surely be able to tell if one were missing, as must have been the case if the gipsies had carried off Anitra before the fire."

"I don't know about that," objected the stone-cutter. "There was, in those days, a little orphan girl, almost an idiot, who wandered about this town, staying now in one house and now in another as folks took compassion on her. She was never seen agin after that fire. If she was in the schoolhouse that day, as she sometimes was, the number would be made up. No one was left to tell us. It was an awful time, sir. The village hasn't got over it yet."

Mr. Ransom made some sympathetic rejoinder and withdrew towards the gateway, but soon came strolling back. The man had arranged his tools and was preparing to go to work.

"It seems as if the family was pretty well represented here," remarked Ransom. "Is it the girl herself,—Anitra, I believe you called her,—who has ordered this record of her death removed?"

"Oh, no, you don't know them Hazens. There's one of 'em who has quite a story; the twin of this Anitra. She lived to grow up and have a lot of money left her. If you lived in Sitford, or lived in New York, you'd know all about her; for her name's been in the papers a lot this week. She's the great lady who married and left her husband all in one day; and for what reason do you think? We know, because she don't keep no secrets from her old friends. She's found this sister, and it's her as has ordered me to chip away this name. She wants it done to-day, because she's coming here with this gal she's found. Folks say she ran across her in the street and knew her at once. Can you guess how?"

"From her name?"

"Lord, no; from what I hear, she hadn't any name. From her looks! She saw her own self when she looked at her."

"How interesting, how very interesting," stammered Mr. Ransom, feeling his newly won convictions shaken again. "Quite remarkable the whole story. And so is this inscription," he added, pointing to the words Georgian Toritti, etc. "Did the woman have two husbands, and was the Alfred Hazen, whose death at sea is commemorated here, the son of Toritti or of Hazen?"

"Of Toritti," grumbled the man, evidently displeased at the question. "A black-browed devil who it won't do to talk about here. Mrs. Hazen was only a slip of a gal when she married him, and as he didn't live but a couple o' months folks have sort o' forgiven her and forgotten him. To us Mrs. Hazen was always Mrs. Hazen; and Alf—well, he was just Alf Hazen too; a lad with too much good in him to perish in them murderous waters a thousand miles from home."

So they still believed Hazen dead! No intimation of his return had as yet reached Sitford. This was what Ransom wanted to know. But there was still much to learn. Should he venture an additional question?

No, that would show more than a stranger's interest in a topic so purely local. Better leave well enough alone and quit the spot before he committed himself.

Uttering some commonplace observation about the fatality attending certain families, he nodded a friendly good-by and made for the entrance.

As he stepped below the brow of the hill he heard the first click of the workman's hammer on the chisel with which he proposed to eliminate the word Anitra from the list of the Hazen dead.

CHAPTER IX

HUNTER'S INN

When Mr. Ransom re-entered the hotel, which he did under a swoop of wind which turned his umbrella inside out and drenched him through in an instant, it was to find the house in renewed turmoil, happily explained by the landlady, whom he ran across on the stairs.

"Oh, Mr. Johnston!" she cried as she edged by him with a pile of bed-linen on her arm. "Please excuse all this fuss. Another guest is coming—I have just got a telegram. A famous lawyer from New York. Our house will be full to-night."

"Where will you put him?" inquired Mr. Ransom with a good-natured air. "There seem to be no unoccupied rooms on this hall."

"More's the pity," she sighed, with a half-inquiring, half deprecatory look at this fortunate first comer. "I shall have to put him below, poor man. I'm afraid he won't like it, but—" Mr. Ransom remained silent. "But," she went on with sudden cheerfulness, "I will make it up in the supper. That shall be as good a one as our kitchen will provide. Four city guests all in one day! That's a good many for this quiet hotel."

"Four!" retorted Mr. Ransom as he turned towards his own door. "The number has grown by two since I went out."

"Oh, I didn't tell you. The lady—her name's Mrs. Ransom—brings her sister with her. The little girl who—yes, I am coming." This latter to some perplexed domestic down the hall, who had already called her twice. "I mustn't stand talking here," she apologized as she hurried away. "But do take care of yourself. You are dreadful wet. How I wish the weather would clear up!"

Mr. Ransom wished the same. To say nothing of his own inconvenience, it was a source of anxiety to him that she should have to ride these inevitable ten miles in such a chilling downpour. Besides, a storm of this kind complicated matters; gave him less sense of freedom, shut him in, as it were, with the mystery he was there to unravel, but which for some reason, hardly explainable to himself, filled him with such a sense of foreboding that he had moments in which he thought only of escape. But his part must be played and he prepared himself to play it well. Having changed his clothes and warmed himself with a draft of whisky, he sat down at his table and was busy writing when the maid came in to ask if he would wait for his supper till the coach came, or have it earlier and served in his own room.

With an air of petulance, he looked up, rapped on the table, and replied:

"Here! here! I'm too busy to meet strangers. An early supper and an early bed. That's the way I get through my work."

The girl stared and went softly out. Work!—that? Sitting at a table and just putting words on paper. If it was beds he had to drag around now, or a dozen hungry, clamoring men to feed all at once, and all with the best cuts, or stairs to run up fifty times a day, or—but I need not fill out her thought. It made her voluble in the kitchen and secured him the privacy which his incognito demanded.

His supper over, he waited feverishly for the coach, which ordinarily was due at seven in the evening. To-night it bade fair to be late, owing to the bad condition of the roads and the early darkness. The wind had gone down, but it still rained. Not quite so tempestuously as when he roamed the cemetery, but steadily enough to keep eaves and branches dripping. The sound of this ceaseless drip was eerie enough to his strained senses, waiting as he was for an event which might determine the happiness or the misery of his life. He tried to forget it and wrote diligently, putting down words whose meaning he did not stop to consider, so that he had something to show to prying eyes if such should ever glance through his papers. But the sound had got on his brain, and presently became so insistent that he rose again and flung his window up to see if he were deceived in thinking he heard a deep roar mingling with the incessant patter, a roar which the wind had hitherto prevented him from separating from the general turmoil, but which now was apparent enough to call for some explanation.

He had made no mistake; a steady sound of rushing water filled the outside air. A fall was near, a fall by means of which, no doubt, the factories were run.

Why had he not thought of this? Why had its sound held a note of menace for him, awakening feelings he did not understand and from which he sought to escape? A factory fall swollen by the rain! What was there in this to make his hand shake and cause the deepening night to seem positively hateful to him? With a bang he closed the window; then he softly threw it up again. Surely he had heard the noise of wheels splashing through the pools of the highway. The coach was coming! and with it—what?

His room was in the gable end facing the road. From it he could look directly down on the porch of entrance, a fact which he had thankfully noted at his first look. As he heard the bustle which now broke out below, and caught the gleam of a lantern coming round the corner of the house, he softly stepped to his lamp and put it out, then took his stand at the window. The coach was now very near; he could hear the straining of the harness and the shouts of the driver. In another moment it drew lumberingly up. A man from the hotel advanced with an umbrella; a young lady was helped out who, standing one moment in the full glare of the lights thrown upon her from the open door, showed him the face and form he knew so well and loved—yes, loved for all her mystery, as he knew by the wild beating of his heart, and the irresistible impulse he felt to rush down and receive her in his arms, to her great terror doubtless, but to his own boundless satisfaction and delight. But strong as the temptation was, he did not yield to it. Something in her attitude, as she stood there, talking earnestly to the driver, held him spellbound and alert. All was not right; there was passion in her movements and in her voice. What she said drew the heads of landlady and maid from the open door and caused the man with the lantern to peer past her into the coach and backward along the road. What had happened? Nothing that concerned the lawyer. Mr. Ransom could see him disentangling himself from the coverings in front where he had ridden with the driver, but the sister was not there. No other lady got out of the coach even after his young wife had finished her conversation with the driver and disappeared into the house.

"How can I stand this?" thought Mr. Ransom as the coach finally rattled and swished away towards the stable. "I must hear, I must see, I must know what is going on down there."

This because he heard voices in the open hall. Crossing to his own doorway, he listened. His wife and Mr. Harper had stepped into the office close by the front door. He could hear now and then a word of what they said, but not all. Venturing a step further, he leaned over the balustrade which extended almost up to his own door. This was better; he could now catch most of the words and sometimes a sentence. They all referred to the sister. "Temper—her own way—deaf—would walk in all the rain and slush—A strange character—you can't imagine," and other similar phrases, uttered in a passionate and half-angry voice. Then ejaculations from Mrs. Deo, and a word or two of caution or injunction in the polished tones of the lawyer, followed by a sudden rush towards the staircase, over which he was leaning.

"Show me my room," rang up in Georgian's bell-like tones; "then I'll tell you what to do about her. She isn't easily managed."

"But she'll get her death!" expostulated Mrs. Deo; "to say nothing of her losing her way in this dreadful darkness. Let me send—"

"Not yet," broke in his young wife's voice, with just the hint of asperity in it. "She must trudge out her tantrum first. I think her idea was to show that she remembered the old place and the lane where she used to pick blackberries. You needn't worry about her getting cold. She's lived a gipsy life too many years to mind wind and wet. But it's different with me. I'm all in a shiver. Which is my room, please?"

She was now at the head of the stairs. Mr. Ransom had closed his door, but not latched it, and as she turned to go down the hall, followed by the chattering landlady, he swung it open for an instant and so caught one full glimpse of her beloved figure. She was dressed in a long rain-coat and had some sort of modish hat on her head, which, in spite of its simplicity, gave her a highly fashionable air. A woman to draw all eyes, but such a mystery to her husband! Such a mystery to all who knew her story, or rather her actions, for no one seemed to know her story.

Events did not halt. He heard her give this and that order, open a door and look in; say a word of commendation, ask if the key was on her side of the partition, then shut the door again and open another.

"Ah, this looks comfortable," she exclaimed in great satisfaction. "Is that my bag? Put it down, please. I'll open it. Now, if you'll leave me a moment alone, I'll soon be ready. But you mustn't expect me to eat till Anitra comes. I couldn't do that. Oh, she's a dreadful trial, Mrs. Deo; you have a motherly face, and I can tell you that the girl is just eating up my life. If she weren't my very self, deafened by hard usage, and rendered coarse and wilful by years of a miserable and half-starved life, I couldn't bear it, especially after what I've sacrificed for her. I've parted with my husband—but I can't talk, I can't. I would not have said so much if you hadn't looked so kind."

All this her husband heard, followed by a sob or two, quickly checked, however, by a high strained laugh and the gay remark:

"I'm wet enough, but she'll be dripping. I'm afraid she'll have to have her supper in her room. She got out at the new schoolhouse and started to come through the lane. It must be a weltering pool. If I'm dressed in time I'll come down and meet her at the door. Meanwhile don't wait for us; give Mr. Harper his supper."

Her door closed, then suddenly opened again. "If she don't come in ten minutes, let some one go to the head of the lane. But be sure it's a careful person who won't startle her. I've got to put on another dress, so don't bother me. I'll hear her when she enters her own room and will speak to her then—if I dare; I'm not sure that I shall." And the door shut to again, this time with a snap of the lock. Quiet reigned once more in the hall save for Mrs. Deo's muttered exclamations as she made her laborious way down-stairs. Had this good woman been less disturbed and not in so much of a hurry, she might have noted that the door of her literary guest's room was ajar, and stopped to ask why the lamp remained unlit.

For five minutes, for ten minutes, he watched and listened, passing continually to and fro from door to window. But his vigilance remained unrewarded by any further movement in the hall, or by the sight of an approaching figure up the road. He began to feel odd, and was asking himself what sort of fool-work this was, when a clatter of voices rose below, followed by heavy steps on the veranda. One or two men were going out, and as it seemed to him the landlady too, for he heard her say just as the door closed:

"Let me on ahead; she must see a woman's kind face first, poor child, or we shall not succeed in getting her in. I know all about these wild ones."

PART II

THE CALL OF THE WATERFALL

CHAPTER X

TWO DOORS

The enthusiasm, the expectation in Mrs. Deo's voice were unmistakable. This good woman believed in this rescued waif of turbulent caprices and gipsy ways, and from this moment he began to believe in her too, and consequently to share some of the excitement which had now become prevalent all through the house.

His suspense was destined to be short. While he was straining his eyes to see what might be going on down the road, a small crowd of people came round the corner of the house. In their midst walked a woman with a shawl or cape over her head—a fierce and wilful figure which shook off the hand kind Mrs. Deo laid on her arm, and shrank as the great front door fell open, sending forth a flood of light which, to one less wedded to wild ways and outdoor living, promised a hospitable cheer.

"Georgian's form!" muttered Ransom involuntarily to himself. "And Georgian's face!" he felt obliged to add, as the light fell broadly across her. "But not Georgian's ways and not Georgian's nature," he impetuously finished as she slipped out of sight.

Then the mystery of the brother came rushing over him and he yielded himself again to the wonder of the situation till he was reawakened to realities by the shuffling of feet on the stairway and the raised tones of Mrs. Deo as she tried to make herself understood by her new and somewhat difficult guest. A maid followed in their wake, and from some as yet unexplored region below there rose the sound of clattering dishes.

It was a trying moment for him. He longed for another glimpse of the girl, but feared to betray his own curiosity to the two women who accompanied her. Should he be forced to allow her to enter her room unseen? Might he not better run some small risk of detection? He had escaped discovery before; wasn't it possible for him to escape it again? He finally compromised matters by first flinging his door wide open and then retreating to the other end of the room where the shadows appeared heavy enough to hide him. From this point he cast a look down the hall which was in a direct line from his present standpoint, and was fortunate enough to catch a glimpse of the girl with her face turned in his direction. Her companions, on the contrary, were standing with their backs to him, one beside the door she had just thrown open, the other at his wife's door on which she had just given a significant rap.

Such was the picture.

The girl absorbed all his attention. The shawl—a gay one with colors in it—had fallen from her head and was trailing, wet and bedraggled, over an equally bedraggled skirt. Soused with wet, her hair disheveled, and all her garments awry with the passion of her movements, she yet made his heart stand still, as, with a sullen look at those about her, she rushed into the room prepared for her use and slammed the door behind her with a quick cry of mingled rage and relief. For with all these drawbacks of manner and appearance she was the living picture of Georgian; so like her, indeed, that he could well understand now the shock which his darling received when, in the unconsciousness of possessing a living sister, she had encountered in street or store, or wherever they had first met, this living reproduction of herself.

"No wonder she became confused as to her duty," he muttered. "I even feel myself becoming confused as to mine."

"Bring me up something to eat," he now heard this latest comer shout from her doorway. "I don't want tea and I don't want soup; I want meat, meat. And I shan't go down afterward, either. I'm going to stay right here. I've seen enough of people I don't know. And of my sister too. She was cross to me because I hated the coach and wanted to walk, and she shan't come into my room till I tell her to. Don't forget; it's meat I want, just meat and something sweet. Pudding's good."

All shocking to Mr. Ransom's taste, but more so to his heart. For notwithstanding the coarseness of the expressions, the voice was Georgian's and laden with a hundred memories.

He was still struggling with the agitation of this discovery when he heard Mrs. Deo give another tap on his wife's door. This time it was unlocked and pushed softly open, and through the crack thus made some whispered orders were given. These seemed to satisfy Mrs. Deo, for she called the maid to her and together they hurried down the hall to a rear staircase, communicating with the kitchen. This was fortunate for him, for if they had turned his way he would have had to issue from his room and take open part in the excitement of the moment.

A few minutes of quiet now supervened. During these he decided that if he must keep up this watch— and nothing now could deter him from doing so—he must take a position consistent with his assumed character. Detection by Georgian was what he now feared. Whatever happened, she must not get the smallest glimpse of him or be led by any indiscretion on his part to suspect his presence under the same roof as herself. Yet he must see all, hear all that was possible to him. For this a continuance of the present conditions, an open door and no light, were positively requisite. But how avert the comment which this unusual state of things must awaken if noticed? But one expedient suggested itself. He would light a cigar and sit in the window. If questioned he would say that he was engaged in deciding how he would end the story he was writing; that such contemplation called for darkness but above all for good air; that had the weather been favorable he would have obtained the latter by opening the window; but it being so bad he could only open the door. Certain eccentricities are allowable in authors.

This settled, he proceeded to take a chair and envelope himself in smoke. With eyes fixed on the dimly-lighted vista of the hall before him, he waited. What would happen next? Would his wife reappear? No; supper was coming up. He could hear dishes rattling on the rear stairway, and in another moment saw the maid coming down the hall with a large tray in her hands. She stopped at Anitra's door, knocked, and was answered by the harsh command:

"Set it down. I'll get it for myself."

The maid set it down.

Next instant Mrs. Ransom's door opened.

"Don't be too generous with me," he heard her call softly out. "I can't eat. I'm too upset for much food. Tea," she whispered, "and some nice toast. Tell Mrs. Deo that I want nothing else. She will understand."

The maid nodded and disappeared down the hall just as a bare arm was thrust out from Anitra's door and the tray drawn in. A few minutes later the other tray came up and was carried into Mrs. Ransom's room. The contrast in the way the two trays had been received struck him as showing the difference between the two women, especially after he had been given an opportunity, as he was later, of seeing the ferocious way in which the food brought to Anitra had been disposed of.

But I anticipate. The latter tray had not yet been pushed again into the hall, and Mr. Ransom was still smoking his first cigar when he heard the lawyer's voice in the office below asking to have pen and ink placed in the small reception-room. This recalled him to the real purpose of his wife's presence in the house, and also assured him that the opportunity would soon be given him for another glimpse of her before the evening was over. It was also likely to be a full-face one, as she would have to advance several steps directly towards him before taking the turn leading to the front staircase.

He awaited the moment eagerly. The hour for signing the will had been set at nine o'clock, but it was surely long past that time now. No, the clock in the office is striking; it is just nine. Would she recognize the summons? Assuredly; for with the last stroke she lifts the latch of her door and comes out.

She has exchanged her dark dress for a light one and has arranged her hair in the manner he likes best. But he scarcely notes these changes in the interest he feels in her intentions and the manner in which she proceeds to carry out her purpose.

She does not advance at once to the staircase, but creeps first to her sister's door, where she stands listening for a minute or so in an attitude of marked anxiety. Then, with a gesture expressive of repugnance and alarm, she steps quickly forward and disappears down the staircase without vouchsafing one glance in his direction.

His vision of her as she looked in that short passage from room to staircase was momentary only, but it left him shuddering. Never before had he seen resolve burning to a white heat in the human countenance. There was something abnormal in it, taken with his knowledge of her face in its happier and more wholesome aspects. The innocent, affectionate young girl, whose soul he had looked upon as a weeded garden, had become in a moment to his eyes a suffering, determined, deeply concentrated woman of unsuspected power and purpose. A suggestion of wildness in her air added to the mysterious impression she made; an impression which rendered this instant memorable to him and set his pulses beating to a tune quite new to them. What was she going to do? Sign away all her property? Beggar her heirs for—He could not say what. No; even such a resolution could not account for her remarkable expression of concentrated will. There was in her distracted mind something of more tragic import than this; and he dared not question what; dared not even approach this woman who, less than a week before, had linked herself to him for life. The uneasy light in those fixed and gleaming eyes betrayed a reason too lightly poised. He feared any additional shock for her. Better that she should go down undisturbed to her adviser, who bore a reputation which insured a judicious use of his power. What if she were about to will away her fortune to the man she called brother? He himself had no use for her wealth. Her health and happiness were all that concerned him, and these possibly depended on her being allowed to go her own way without interference. But oh, for eyes to see into the room into which she had withdrawn with the lawyer! For eyes to see into her heart! For eyes to see into the future!

His suspense presently became so great that he could no longer control himself. Throwing up the window, he thrust his head out into the rain and felt refreshed by the icy drops falling on his face and neck. But the roar of the waterfall rang too persistently in his ears and he hastily closed the window again. There was something in the incessant boom of that tumbling water which strangely disturbed him. He could better stand suspense than that. If only the wind would bluster again. That, at least, was intermittent in its fury and gave momentary relief to thoughts strained to an unbearable tension.

Afterwards, only a short time afterwards, he wondered that he had given himself over to such extreme feeling at this especial moment. Her appearance when she came quietly back, with Mrs. Deo chatting and smiling behind her, was natural enough, and though she did not speak herself, the tenor of the landlady's remarks was such as to show that they had been conversing about old days when the two little girls used to ransack her cupboards for their favorite cookies, and when their united pranks were the talk of the town.

As they passed down the hall, Mrs. Deo garrulously remarked:

"You were never separated except on that dreadful day of the schoolhouse burning. That day you were sick and—"

"Please!" The word leaped from Georgian in terror, and she almost threw her hand against the other's mouth. "I—I can't bear it."

The good lady paused, gurgled an apology, and stooped for the tray which disfigured the sightliness of the neatly kept hall. Then, nodding towards a maid whom she had placed on watch at the extreme end of the hall, she muttered some assurances as to this woman's faithfulness, and turned away with a cordial good night. Georgian watched her go with a strange and lingering intentness, or so it seemed to Ransom; then slowly entered her room and locked the door.

The incidents of the day, so far as she was concerned, appeared to be at an end.

CHAPTER XI

HALF-PAST ONE IN THE MORNING

Nothing now held Mr. Ransom to his room. The two women in whose fate he was so nearly concerned, his sister-in-law and his wife, had both retired and there was no other eye he feared. Indeed, he courted an interview with the lawyer, if only it could be naturally obtained; and he had little reason to think it could not. So he went down-stairs.

In a moment he seemed to have passed from the realm of dreams to that of reality. Here was no mystery. Here was life as he knew it. Walking boldly into the office, he ran his eye over the half-dozen men who sat there and, picking out the lawyer from the rest, sauntered easily up to him and sat down.

"My name is Johnston," said he. "I'm from New York; like yourself, I believe."

The lawyer, with a twinkle in his light-blue eye, answered with a cordial nod; and in two minutes a lively conversation had begun between them on purely impersonal subjects suited to the intelligence of the crowd they were in. This did not last, however. An opportunity soon came for them to stroll off together, and presently Mr. Ransom found himself closeted with this man who he had reason to believe was the sole holder of the key to the secret which was devouring him.

A bottle of wine was on the table between them, and some cigars. As Mr. Ransom filled the two glasses, he spoke:

"I have to thank you—" he began, but saw immediately that he had made a wrong start.

"For what, Mr. Johnston?" asked the other coldly.

"For giving me this opportunity to speak alone with you," Ransom explained with a nervous gesture. "An hour of unrestrained gossip is so necessary to me after a day of hard work. Perhaps you don't know that I am an author—have been one for seven whole hours. I find it exhausting. You could give me great relief by talking a little on some foreign subject, say on the one now engrossing every one in the house, the twin ladies from New York. You were in the same coach with them. Did they quarrel and did the most wilful of the two insist on getting out at the foot of the hill and walking up through the lane?"

"I doubt if I have anything to say to Mr. Johnston on this subject," was the wary reply.

"What if he added another name to the Johnston?"

"It would make no appreciable difference. The driver is a loquacious fellow, talk to him."

Mr. Ransom felt his heart fail him. He surveyed closely the mouth which had uttered this off-hand sentence and saw that it was set in a line there was no mistaking. Little enlightenment was to be got from this man. Yet he made one more effort.

"Did my wife sign the will?" he asked. "All pretense aside, this is a very important matter to me, Mr. Harper; not on account of the money involved, but because the doing of this simple act seemed to require such an effort on her part."

"You are mistaken," was the quick reply, harshly accentuated. "She did just what she wanted to do. She was not in the least coerced, unless it was by circumstances."

"Circumstances! But that is what I mean. They seem to have been too much for her. I want to understand these circumstances."

The lawyer honored him with his first direct look.

"I don't understand them myself," said he.

"You don't?"

"No."

Mr. Ransom set down the wineglass he had raised half-way to his lips.

"You have simply followed her orders?"

"You have said it. Your wife is a woman of much more character than you think. She has amazed me."

"She is amazing me. I am here; she is here; only a few boards separate us. But iron bars could not be more effectual. I dare not approach her door; dare not ask her to accept from me the natural protection of a lover and husband. Instinct holds me back, or her will, which may not be stronger than mine but is certainly more dominant."

"Lawyers do not believe much in instinct as a usual thing, but I should advise confidence in this one. A woman with a tremendous will like that of Mrs. Ransom should be allowed a slack tether. The day will arrive when she will come to you herself. This I have said before; I can say nothing more to you to-night."

"Then there is nothing in the will you have drawn up to show that she has lost her affection for me?"

The lawyer drained his glass.

"I have not been given permission to declare its terms," said he, when his glass was again upon the table.

"In other words, I am to know nothing," exclaimed his exasperated companion.

"Not from me."

And this ended the conversation. Ransom withdrew immediately up-stairs.

At ten o'clock he retired. The last look he cast down the hall had shown him the drowsy figure of the maid still sitting at her watch. It seemed to insure a peaceful night. But he had little expectation of sleep. Though the wind had quieted down and the rain fell with increasing gentleness, the roar of the waterfall surged through all his thoughts, which in themselves were turbulent. He did sleep, however, slept peacefully till half-past one, when he and all in the house were startled by a wild and piercing cry rising from one of the rooms. Terror was in the sound and in an instant every door was open save the two which were shut upon Georgian and her twin sister.

CHAPTER XII

"GEORGIAN!"

Mr. Ransom was the first one in the hall. He had not undressed himself, expecting a totally sleepless night. It was his figure, then, that the maid encountered as she came running from her post at the end of the corridor.

"Which room? which?" he gasped out, ignoring every precaution in his blind terror.

"This one. I am sure it came from this one," she declared, knocking loudly on Anitra's door.

There was a rustle within, a cry which was half a sob, then the sound of a hand fumbling with the lock. Meanwhile, Mr. Ransom had bent his ear to his wife's door.

"All still in here," he cried. "Not a sound. Something dreadful has happened—"

Just then Anitra's door fell back and a wild image confronted him and such others as had by this time collected in the passageway. With only a shawl covering her nightdress, the gipsy-like creature stood clawing the air and answering the looks that appealed to her, with wild gurgles, till suddenly her hot glances fell on Roger Ransom, when she instantly became rigid and stammered out:

"She's gone! I saw her black figure go by my window. She called out that the waterfall drew her. She went by the little balcony and the roof. The roof was slippery with the rain and she fell. That's why I screamed. But she got up again. What is she going to do at the waterfall? Stop her! stop her! She hasn't steady feet like me, and I wasn't really angry. I liked her; I liked her."

Sobs choked the rest. Her terror was infectious. Mr. Ransom reeled, then flung himself at Georgian's door. It resisted but the silence within told him that she was not there. Neither was she in Anitra's room. They could all look in and see it bare to the window.

"You saw her climbing past there?" he cried, forgetting she was deaf.

"Yes, yes," she chattered, catching his meaning from his pointing finger. "There's a balcony. She must have jumped on it from her own window. She didn't come in here. See! the door is locked on her side."

This was true.

"I woke and saw her. My eyes are like lynx's. I got out of bed to watch. She fell—"

The noise of a breaking lock snapped her words in two. One of the men present had flung himself against this communicating door. Immediately they all crowded into the adjoining room. It was empty and bitterly cold and wet. An open window explained why, and possibly the letter lying on the bureau inscribed with her husband's name would explain the rest. But he stopped to read no letters now.

"Show me the way to those falls," he cried, pocketing the letter as he rushed by the disheveled Anitra into the open hall. "I'm her husband, Roger Ransom. Who goes with me? He who does is my friend for life."

The clerk and one or two others rushed for their coats and lanterns. He waited for nothing. The roar of the waterfall had told him too many tales that day. And the will! Her will just signed!

"Georgian!"

They could hear his cry.

"Georgian! Georgian! Wait! wait! hear what I have to say!" thrilled back through the mist as he stumbled on, followed by the men waving their lanterns and shouting words of warning he probably never heard. Then his cry further off and fainter. "Georgian! Georgian!" Then silence and the slow drizzle of rain on the soggy walk and soaked roofs, with the far-off boom of the waterfall which Mrs. Deo and the trembling maids gazing at the wide-eyed Anitra shivering in the center of her deserted room, tried to shut out by closing window and blind, forgetting that she was deaf and only heard such echoes as were thundering in her own mind.

CHAPTER XIII

WHERE THE MILL STREAM RUNS FIERCEST

Two o'clock.

Three o'clock.

Two men were talking below their breaths in the otherwise empty office. "That 'ere mill stream never gives up anything it has once caught," muttered one into the ear of the other. "It's swift as fate and in certain places deep as hell. Dutch Jan's body was five months at the bottom of it, before it came up at Clark's pool."

The man beside him shivered and his hand roamed nervously towards his breast.

"Did Jan, the Dutchman you speak of, fall in by accident, or did he—throw himself over—from homesickness, or some such cause?"

"Wa'al we don't say; on account of his old mother, you know, we don't say. It was called accident."

The other man rose and walked restlessly to the window.

"Half the town is up," he muttered. "The lanterns go by like fire-flies. Poor Ransom! It's a hopeless job, I fear." And again his hand wandered to that breast pocket where the edge of a document could be seen. "I have half a mind to go out myself; anything is better than sitting here."

But he sat down just the same. Mr. Harper was no longer a young man.

"The storm's bating," observed the one.

"But not the cold. Throw on a stick; I'm freezing."

The other man obeyed; then looking up, stared. A girl stood before them in the doorway. Anitra, with cheeks ablaze and eyes burning, her traveling dress flapping damp about her heels, and on her head the red shawl she preferred to any hat. Behind her shoulder peered the anxious face of Mrs. Deo.

"I'm going out," cried the former in the loud and unmodulated voice of the deaf. "He don't come back! he don't come back! I'm going to see why."

The lawyer rose and bowed; then resolutely shook his head. He did not know whether she had appealed to him or not. She had not looked at him, had not looked at any one, but he felt that he must protest.

"I beg you not to do so," he began. "I really beg you to remain here and wait with me. You can do no good and the result may be dangerous." But he knew he was talking to deaf ears even before the landlady murmured:

"She doesn't hear a word. I've talked and talked to her. I've used every sign and motion I could think of, but it's done no good. She would dress and she will go out; you'll see."

The next minute her prophecy came true; the wild thing, with a quick whirl of her lithe body, was at the front door, and in another instant had flashed through it and was gone.

"It is my duty to follow her," said the lawyer. "Help me on with my coat; I'll find some one to guide me."

"Here is a lantern. Excuse me for not going with you," pleaded Mrs. Deo, "but some one must watch the house."

The New Yorker nodded, took the lantern offered him, and went stoically out.

He met a man on the walk in front. He was faced his way and was panting heavily.

"Hello," said he, "what news?"

"They haven't found her; but there's no doubt she went over the fall. The fellow who calls himself her husband has just been reading a letter they say she left on her bureau for him. It was a good-by, I reckon, for you can't tear him from the spot. He says he'll stay there till daylight. I couldn't stand the sight of his misery myself. Besides, it's mortal cold; I've just been running to get warm. Who was the girl who just went scurrying by out of here? It's no place for wimmen down there. One lost gal is enough."

"That's what I think," muttered the lawyer, hurrying on.

He was not a very imaginative man; some of his best friends thought him a cold and prosaic one, but he never forgot that walk or the sensations accompanying it. Dark as it still was, the way would have been impassable for a stranger, had it not been for the guidance given by the noisy passing to and fro of the awakened townspeople. Those coming from the river approached in a direct line from one spot; those going to it advanced in the same line and to the same spot. A ring of lanterns marked it. It was near, very near where the heavy waters fell into a deep pool. No one now spoke of Anitra; she had evidently been warned by her first encounter to move with less precipitancy.

As he approached the place of central interest, he moved more warily too. The ground was very bad; he had never walked in such slush. Once and again he tripped; once he came down upon his face. The boom of the waters was now very near; he could see nothing but the flicker of the lanterns, but he felt the near rush of the stream, and presently was at its very edge. Startled by the nearness of his escape, for he had almost lost his footing by his sudden halt, he started back, looked again at the lanterns, took a turn and came upon the dozen or more men bending over the edge of the stream where the waters ran most swiftly. But he did not join them. Another sight attracted his eyes and presently himself. This was the sight of Ransom crouched on the wet earth, staring down at a slip of paper he held in his hands. A lantern set in the sand at his feet sent its feeble rays over his face and possibly over the paper; but he was no longer reading it, he was simply so lost in its sorrowful contents that all power of movement had deserted him.

Harper approached to his side, but he did not address him. Something stirred in his own breast and kept him silent. But there was another person near who was not so deterred. As Harper stood watching Ransom's crouched, almost insensible figure, he perceived a slight dark form steal from the shadows and lay a hand on the stooping man's shoulder, then as he failed to move or give any token of feeling this touch, he heard Anitra's voice say in accents almost musical:

"You will get ill here; you are not used to the cold and the night air. Come back to the house; Georgian would wish it."

The name roused him and he looked up. Their eyes met and a strange gleam—a shock, perhaps, of sympathetic feeling, flashed upon either face. The lawyer saw and instinctively retreated from out the circle of light cast by the lantern; but the men at the stream's edge heard nothing. The flash of something white had caught their eyes and one man was reaching for it.

"Georgian," came in astonished repetition from the bereaved man's lips.

"She would wish it," persisted the other with still deeper and more urgent meaning.

Then in a whisper so penetrating that even Mr. Harper caught its least inflection through all the thunder of the waterfall, "She loved you."

Ah! the enchantment, the feminine persuasiveness, the heart-moving sincerity which breathed through that simple phrase! From lips so untutored, it seemed marvelous. Ransom was not insensible to its power, for he quivered under her hand and his eyes took on a look of wonder. But he made no attempt to answer, even by a sign. He seemed content for that one instant just to listen and to look.

The man hanging over the stream drew back his arm. He had been deceived by a bit of froth; some of it clung yet to his fingers.

"Come," entreated the girl, her face emerging softly into the light, as she stooped lower over the lantern. "Come!" she had taken him by the hand and was drawing him gently upward.

With a leap he was on his feet and had thrown her off. Some memory had come to make her entreaty hateful.

"No," he cried, "no! Here is my place and here will I stay. You are a stranger to me! You drove her to this act, and you shall not cajole me into forgetting it."

He had spoken loudly; not so much because he remembered her affliction, but because of the roar of the fall and his own overwhelming passion. The result was that the lawyer caught every word; possibly the workers at the water-edge did also; for some of them quickly turned their heads. But she, though she stopped short in the spot where he had pushed her, gave no evidence of hearing his words or even of resenting his manner.

"Won't you come?" she falteringly pleaded, pointing towards the house with its twinkling lights. "You are cold; you are shuddering; they will do the searching who don't mind night or wet. Follow Anitra, Anitra who is so sorry."

"No!" he shouted. His tone, his look, were almost those of a madman. He even put out his hands towards her in repulsion. He seemed to cast her away. This gesture, if not his words, reached her understanding. The lawyer saw her sway, fling back her young head with its disheveled locks to the night, and fall moaning pitifully to the ground. Here she lay still, with the wet grass all about her and the last lingering drops of rain beating on her huddled form.

Mr. Harper started to raise her, for Ransom stood petrified. But no sooner had the lawyer made his presence known by this impetuous movement, than Ransom woke from his trance and, darting down, lifted the girl in his arms and began moving with her towards the house. As he passed the lawyer he muttered between set teeth:

"She's caused me all my misery. But she looks too much like Georgian for me to see another man touch her. God will care for my poor darling's body."

CHAPTER XIV

A DETECTIVE'S WORK

Morning.

The living household was about its tasks for all the horror of the night before, and the still unrelieved suspense as to the fate of one of its members.

The maid, who had sat on watch in the upper hall for so many hours the evening before, was again at her post, but this time with her eye fixed only on one door, the door behind which slept the exhausted Anitra. Ransom's room was empty; he was in the sitting-room below, closeted with the lawyer.

Some one had been there before them. The tray of bottles and glasses had been removed from the table, and in their place were to be seen a woman's damaged hat and a small tortoise-shell comb. Mr. Harper's hand was on the former, which was wound about with a wet veil.

"I think I recognize this," said he. "At least I have a distinct impression of having seen it before."

"It was picked up with the veil still on it near the entrance of the lane," explained Ransom.

"Then there can be no doubt that it is the hat Miss Hazen wore during her journey. She tossed it off the moment her foot touched the ground, and taking the shawl from her neck pulled it over her head instead. You remember that she had no hat on when they brought her in."

"I remember. This is Miss Hazen's hat without any doubt."

The lawyer eyed the speaker with curious interest. There was something in his tone that he did not understand.

"And this?" he ventured, laying a respectful finger on the comb.

"Found in the open field between the house and the mill-stream."

"Do you recognize it?"

"No. Georgian wore such combs, but I cannot absolutely say that this is hers."

"I can. You see this little gold work at the top? Well, I have an eye for such things and I noticed this comb in her hair last night. There were two of them just alike."

Instinctively the two men sat with their eyes fixed for a minute on this comb, then, equally instinctively, they both looked up and gazed at each other long and hard. It was the lawyer who first spoke.

"I think that we should have no further secrets between us," said he. "Here is Mrs. Ransom's will. There is a name mentioned in it which I do not know. Perhaps you do." Here he laid the document on the table.

Mr. Ransom eyed it but did not take it up. Instead, he drew a crumpled paper from his own pocket and, handing it to the lawyer, said: "First, I should like you to read the letter which she left behind for me. My feelings as a husband would lead me to hold it as a sacred legacy from all eyes but my own; but there is a mystery hidden in it, a mystery which I must penetrate, and you are the only man who can assist me in doing so."

The lawyer, lowering his eyes to hide their own suspicious glint, opened the paper, and carefully read these lines:

"Forgive. My troubles are too much for me. I'm going to a place of rest, the only place and the only rest possible to one in my position. I don't blame anybody. Least of all do I blame Anitra. It was not her fault that she was brought up rudely, or that she knows no restraint in love or in hate. Be kind to her for my sake, and if any one else claims her or offers to take her from you, resist them. I give her entirely to you. It's a more priceless gift than you think; much more priceless than the one which I take from you by my death. I could never have been happy with you; you could never have been happy with me. Fate stood between us; a darker and more inexorable fate than you, in your kindly experience of life, could imagine. Else, why do I plunge to my death with your ring on my finger and your love in my heart?

"Georgian."

"Ravings?" questioned Ransom hoarsely, as Mr. Harper's eyes rose again to his face.

"It would seem so," assented the lawyer. "Yet there is intelligence in all the lines. And the will—read the will. There is no lack of intelligent purpose there; little as it accords with the feeling she exhibits here for her sister. She leaves her nothing; and does not even mention her name. Her personal belongings she bequeaths to you; but her realty, which comprises the bulk of her property I believe, she divides, somewhat unequally I own, between you and a man named Auchincloss. It is he I want to ask you about. Have you ever heard her speak of him?"

"Josiah Auchincloss of St. Louis, Missouri," read Mr. Ransom. "No, the name is new to me. Didn't she tell you anything about him when she gave you her instructions?"

"Not a word. She said, 'You will hear from him if ever this will is published. He has a right to the money and I entreat you to show your respect for me by seeing that he gets it without any unnecessary trouble.' That was all she said or would say. Your wife was a woman of powerful character, Mr. Ransom. My little arts counted for nothing in any difference of opinion between us."

"Auchincloss!" repeated Ransom. "Another unknown quantity in the problem of my poor girl's life. What a tangle! Do you wonder that I am overcome by it? Anitra—the so-called brother—and now this Auchincloss!"

"Right, Ransom, I share your confusion."

"Do you?" The words came very slowly, penetratingly. "Haven't you some idea—some strange, possibly half-formed notion or secret intuition which might afford some clew to this labyrinth? I have been told that lawyers have a knack of getting at the bottom of human conduct and affairs. You have had a wide experience; does it not suggest some answer to this problem which will harmonize all its discordant elements and make clear its various complications?"

Mr. Harper shook his head, but there was a restrained excitement in his manner which was not altogether the reflection of that which dominated Ransom, and the latter, observing it, leaned across the table till their faces almost touched.

"Do you guess my thought?" he whispered. "Look at me and tell me if you guess my thought."

The lawyer hesitated, eying well the trembling lip, the changing color, the wide-open, deeply flushed eyes so near his own; then with a slow smile of extraordinary subtlety, if not of comprehension, answered in a barely audible murmur:

"I think I do. I may be mad, but I think I do."

The other sank back with a sigh charged with what the lawyer interpreted as relief. Mr. Harper reseated himself, and for a moment neither looked at the other, and neither spoke; it would almost seem as if neither breathed. Then, as a bird, deceived by the silence, hopped to the window sill and began its cheep, "cheep," Mr. Ransom broke the spell by saying in low but studiously business-like tones:

"Have you thought it worth while to study the ground under her window or anywhere else for footprints? It might not be amiss; what do you think about it?"

"Let us go," readily acquiesced the lawyer, rising to his feet with an honest show of alacrity; "after which I must telegraph to New York. I was expected back to-day."

"I know it; but your duties there will keep; these here cannot. Your hand on the promise that you will respect my secret till—well, till I can assure you that my intuitions are devoid of any real basis."

The lawyer's palm met his; then they started to go out; but before they had passed the door, Mr. Ransom came back, and lifting the comb from the table he put it in his pocket. As he did this, his eye flashed sidewise on the other. There were strange hints and presentiments in it which brought the color to the usually imperturbable lawyer's cheek.

In going out they passed the office-door. A dozen men were hanging about, smoking and talking. Among them was a countryman who had just swallowed, open-mouthed, the story of the past night's tragedy. He was now speaking out his own mind concerning it, and this is what these two heard him say as they went by:

"Do you know what strikes me as mighty strange? That they should clear that stone of the name of Anitra just in time to put Georgian's in its place. I call that peculiar, I do."

The lawyer and the husband exchanged a glance.

"Mrs. Ransom had a deep mind," the lawyer remarked, as the door slammed behind them. "She apparently thought of everything."

Ransom, directing a look down the street towards the factories and the roaring mill-stream, uttered a shuddering sigh.

"They are still searching," said he. "But they will never find her. They will never find her."

The lawyer pulled him away.

"That's because they search the water. We will search the land."

"That's half water, too; but it cannot hide every clew. You have eyes for the imperceptible; use them, Mr. Harper, use them."

"I will; but this is a detective's work. Do not expect too much from me."

"I expect nothing. I do not dare to. Let us tread very softly, that is all, and be careful to talk low, if we have anything to say."

By this time they had rounded the corner of the house and entered a narrow walk, flagged with brick, which connected the space in front with the rear offices and garden. This walk ran close to the walls which were broken on this side by an ell projecting in the direction of the mill-stream. It was from the roof of this ell that Anitra declared Georgian to have slipped and fallen.

Their first care was to glance up at the roof. It was a sloping one and Anitra's story seemed credible enough when they noted how much easier it would be to drop upon it from the little balcony overhead than to traverse the roof itself and reach the ground beneath without slipping. But as they looked longer, each face betrayed doubt. The descent from the balcony was easy enough, but how about the passage from Georgian's window to the balcony? This latter was confined to the one window, and was surrounded by an ornamental balustrade, high enough to offer a decided obstacle to the adventurous person endeavoring to leap upon it from the adjoining window-ledge. However, this leap, made in the dark and under circumstances inducing the utmost recklessness, might look practical enough from the window-ledge itself, and Mr. Harper, making a remark to this effect, proposed that they should examine the ground rather than the house for evidences of Mrs. Ransom's slip and fall as related by Anitra.

The only spot where they could hope to find such was in the one short stretch—the width of the ell— underlying the edge of the sloping roof. But this spot was all flagged, as I have already said, and when their eyes strayed beyond it to the untilled fields, stretching between them and the great rock at the verge of the waterfall from which she was supposed to have taken her fatal leap, it was to find them as unproductive of evidence as the brick walk itself. Not one pair of feet but many had passed that way since early morning. The ground showed a mass of impressions of all sizes and shapes, amid which it would have been impossible for them, without the necessary experience, to have followed up the flight of any one person. They had come to their task too late.

"Futile," decided the lawyer. "There is no use in our going that way." And he turned to look again at the ground in their immediate vicinity. As he did so, his eye lighted on the triangular spot where the ell met the side of the house under the kitchen windows. Here there was no flagging, the walk taking a diagonal course from the corner of the ell to the kitchen door.

"What are those?" he asked, pointing to two oblong impressions brimming with water which disfigured the center of this small plot.

"They look like footprints," ventured Ransom.

"They are footprints," decided Mr. Harper as they stooped to examine the marks, "and the footprints of a person dropping from a height. Nothing else explains their depth or general appearance."

"Couldn't they be those of a person approaching the ell to converse with some one above? I see others similar to these in the open place over there beyond the kitchen door."

"It is a trail. Let us follow it. It seems to lead anywhere but towards the waterfall. This is an important discovery, Mr. Ransom, and may lead to conclusions such as we might not otherwise have presumed to entertain, especially if we come upon an impression clear enough to point in which direction the person making it was going."

"Here is what you want," Ransom assured him in a low and curiously smothered voice. He was evidently greatly excited by this result of their inquiries, for all his apparent quiet and precise movements. "It's a woman's step, and that woman was going from the ell when she left these tokens of her passage behind her. Going! and as you say not in the direction of the waterfall."

"Hush! I see some one at the kitchen window. Let us move warily and be sure not to confound these prints with those of any other person. It looks as if a great many people had passed here."

"Yes, this is the way to the chicken-coops and out-houses. But in the ground beyond I think I see a single line of steps again,—small steps like these. Where can they be leading? They are deep like those of a person running."

"And straggling, like those of a person running in the dark. See how they waver from the direct line down there, turn, and almost come up against that wood-pile! Whose steps are these? Whose, Mr. Harper? Quick! I must see where they go. Our time will not be lost. The key to the labyrinth is in our hands."

The lawyer was in the rear and the eyes of the other were fixed far ahead. For this reason, perhaps, the former allowed himself a quiet shake of the head, which might not have encouraged the other so very much, had he caught sight of it. They were now on the verge of the garden, or what would soon be a garden if these rains betokened spring. A path ran along its edge and in this path the footsteps they were following lost themselves; but they came upon them again among the hillocks of some old potato-hills beyond, and finally traced them quite across the garden waste to a fence, along which they ran, blundering from ploughed earth to spots of smoother ground, and so back again till they came upon an old turn-stile!

Passing through this, the two men stopped and looked about them. They were in a road ridged with grass and flanked by bushes. One end ran east into a wooded valley, the other debouched on the highway a few feet to the right of the tavern.

"The lane!" exclaimed Mr. Harper. "The lead towards the waterfall was a feint. It was in this direction she fled, and it is from this point that search must be made for her."

Ransom, greatly perturbed, for this possibility of secret flight opened vistas of as much mystery, if not of as much suffering, as her death in the river, glanced at the sodden ground under their feet, and thus along the lane to where it lost itself from view among the trees.

"No possible following of steps here," he declared. "A hundred people must have come this way since early morning."

"It's a short cut from the Ferry. They told me last night that it lessened the distance by fully a quarter of a mile."

"The Ferry! Can she be there? Or in the woods, or on her way to some unknown place far out of our reach? The thought is maddening, Mr. Harper, and I feel as helpless as a child under it. Shall we get detectives from the county-seat, or start on the hunt ourselves? We might hear something further on to help us."

"We might; but I should rather stay on the immediate scene at present. Ah, there comes a fellow in a cart who should be able to tell us something! Stand by and I'll accost him. You needn't show your face."

Mr. Ransom turned aside. Mr. Harper waited till the slow-moving horse, dragging a heavily jogging wagon, came alongside, and he had caught the eye of the low-browed, broad-faced farmer boy who sat on a bag of potatoes and held the reins.

"Good morning," said he. "Bad news this way. Any better at the Ferry, or down east, as you call it?"

"Eh?" was the lumbering, half-suspicious answer from the startled boy. "I've heard naught down yonder, but that a gal threw herself over the waterfall up here last night. Is that a fact, sir? I'm mighty curus to know. My mother knew them Hazens; used to wash for 'em years ago. She told me to bring up these taters and larn all I could about it."

"We don't know much more than that ourselves," was the smooth and cautious reply. "The lady certainly is missing, and she is supposed to have drowned herself." Then, as he noted the fellow's eyes resting with some curiosity on Mr. Ransom's well-clad, gentlemanly figure, added gravely, and with a slight gesture towards the latter:

"The lady's husband."

The lad's jaw fell and he looked very sheepish.

"Excuse me, misters, I didn't know," he managed to mutter, with a slash at his horse which was vainly endeavoring to pull the cart from the rut in which it had stuck. "I guess I'll go along to the hotel. I've a bag of taters for Mrs. Deo."

But the cart didn't budge and the lawyer had time to say:

"Guess you didn't hear anything said about another lady I am interested in. No talk down your way of a strange young woman seen anywhere on the highway or about any of the houses between here and the Landing?"

"Jerusha! I did hear a neighbor of mine say somethin' about a stranger gal he saw this very mornin'. Met her down by Beardsley's. She was goin' through the mud on foot as lively as you please. Asked him the way to the Ferry. He noticed her because she was pretty and spoke in such a nice way—just like a city gal," he said. "Is it any one from this hotel?" added the fellow with a wondering look. "If so, she walked a mile before daylight in mud up to her ankles. A girl of powerful grit that! with a mighty good reason for catching the train."

"Oh! there's an early train then?" asked the lawyer, ignoring the other's question with unmoved good-humor. "One, I mean, before the 10:50 express?"

"Yes, sir, or so I've heard. I never took it. Folks don't from here, except they're in an awful hurry. Will y'er say who the young woman is? Not—not—"

"We don't know who she is," quietly objected the lawyer. "And you don't know who she is either," he severely added, holding the yawping countryman with his eye. "If you're the man I think you, you'll not talk about her unless you're asked by the constable or some one you are bound to answer. And what's more, you'll earn a five-dollar bill by going back the road you've come and bringing here, without any talk or fuss, the man you were just telling us about. I want to have a talk with him, but I don't want any one but you and him to know this. You can tell him it's worth money, if he don't want to come. Do you understand?"

"You bet," chuckled the grinning lad. "A five-dollar bill is mighty clearing to the mind, sir. But must I turn right back before going on to the hotel and hearing the news?"

"We'll help you turn the cart," grimly suggested Mr. Harper. "Get up there, Dobbin, or whatever your name is. Here, Ransom, lend a hand!"

There was nothing for the fellow to do but to accept the help proffered, and turn his cart. With one longing look towards the hotel he jerked at the rein and shouted at the horse, which, after a few feeble efforts, pulled the cart about and started off again in the desired direction.

"Sooner done, sooner paid," shouted the lawyer, as lad and cart went jolting off. "Remember to ask for Lawyer Harper when you come back. I won't be far from the office."

The fellow nodded; gave one grinning look back and whipped up his nag. The lawyer and Ransom eyed one another. "It's only a possibility," emphasized the former. "Don't lay too much stress upon it."

"Let us speak plainly," urged Ransom. "Mr. Harper, are you sure that you know just what my thought is?"

"The time has not come for discussing that question. Let us defer it. There is a fact to be settled first."

"Whether the girl—"

"No; this! Whether your wife could have jumped from her window to the balcony, as Anitra said. It did not look feasible from below, but as I then remarked to you, our opinion may change when we consider it from above. Will you go up-stairs with me to your wife's room?"

"I will go anywhere and do anything you please, so that we learn the exact truth. But spare me the curiosity of these people. The crowd on this side is increasing."

"We will go in by the kitchen door. Some one there will show us the way up-stairs."

And in this manner they entered; not escaping entirely all curious looks, for human nature is human nature, whether in the kitchen or parlor.

In the hall above Mr. Ransom took the precedence. As they neared the fatal room he motioned the lawyer to wait till he could ascertain if Miss Hazen would be disturbed by their intrusion. The door, which had been broken in between the two rooms, could not have been put back very securely, and he dreaded incommoding her. He was gone but a minute. Almost as soon as the lawyer started to follow him, he could be seen beckoning from poor Georgian's door.

"Miss Hazen is asleep," whispered Ransom, as the other drew near. "We can look about this room with impunity."

They both entered and the lawyer crossed at once to the window.

"Your wife could never have taken the leap ascribed to her by the woman you call Anitra," he declared, after a minute's careful scrutiny of the conditions. "The balustrade of the adjoining balcony is not only in the way, but the distance is at least five feet from the extreme end of this window-ledge. A woman accustomed to a life of adventure or to the feats of a gymnasium might do it, but not a lady of Mrs. Ransom's habits. If your wife made her way from this room to the balcony outside her sister's window, she did it by means of the communicating door."

"But the door was found locked on this side. There is the key in the lock now."

"You are sure of this?"

"I was the first one to call attention to it."

"Then," began the lawyer judicially, but stopped as he noted the peculiar eagerness of Ransom's expression, and turned his attention instead to the interior of the room and the various articles belonging to Mrs. Ransom which were to be seen in it. "The dress your wife wore when she signed her will," he remarked, pointing to the light green gown hanging on the inside of the door by which they had entered.

Ransom stepped up to it, but did not touch it. He could see her as she looked in this gown in her memorable passage through the hall the evening before, and, recalling her expression, wondered if they yet understood the nature of her purpose and the determination which gave it such extraordinary vigor.

Mr. Harper called his attention to two other articles of dress hanging in another part of the room. These were her long gray rain-coat and the hat and veil she had worn on the train.

"She went out bare-headed and in the plain serge dress in which she arrived," remarked Mr. Harper with a side glance at Ransom. "I wonder if the girl met on the highway was without hat and dressed in black serge."

Ransom was silent.

"Anitra's hat is below and here is Mrs. Ransom's. She who escaped from this house last night went out bare-headed," repeated the lawyer.

Mr. Ransom, moving aside to avoid the probing of the other's eye, merely remarked:

"You noticed my wife's dress very particularly it seems. It was of serge, you say."

"Yes. I am learned in stuffs. I remarked it when she got into the coach, possibly because I was struck by its simplicity and conventional make. There was no trimming on the bottom, only stitching. Her sister's was just like it. They had the look of being ready-made."

"But Anitra had no rain-coat. I remember that her shoulders were wet when she came in from the lane."

"No, she had no protection but her blouse, black like her dress. I presume that her hot blood resented every kind of wrap."

Again that sidelong glance from his keen eye. "She wore a checked silk handkerchief about her neck— the one she afterwards put over her head."

"You were on the same train with my wife and sister-in-law," Ransom now said. "Did you sit near them? Converse with them, that is, with Mrs. Ransom?"

"I have no reason for deceiving you in that regard," replied Mr. Harper. "I did not come up from New York on the same train they did. They must have come up in the morning, for when I arrived at the place they call the Ferry, I saw them standing on the hotel steps ready to step into the coach. I spoke to Mrs. Ransom then, but only a word. My grip-sack had been put under the driver's seat, and I saw that I was expected to ride with him, notwithstanding the inclemency of the weather. Mrs. Ransom saw it too and possibly my natural hesitation, for she turned to me after she had seen her sister safely ensconced inside, and said something about her regret at having subjected me to such inconvenience, but did not offer to make room for me in the body of the coach, though there was room enough if the other had been the quiet lady she was herself. But she was not, and possibly this was Mrs. Ransom's excuse for her apparent lack of consideration for me. Before we reached the point where the lane cuts in, I became aware of some disturbance behind me, and when we really got there, I heard first the coach door opening, then your wife's voice, raised in entreaty to the driver, calling on him to stop before her sister jumped out and hurt herself. 'She is deaf and very wild' was all the explanation she gave after Miss Hazen had leaped into the wet road and darted from sight into what looked to me, in the darkness, like a tangled mass of bushes. Then she said something about her having had hard work to keep her still till we got this far; but that she was sure she would find her way to the hotel, and that we mustn't bother ourselves about it for she wasn't going to; Anitra and she had run this road too many times when they were children. That is all I have to tell of my intercourse with these ladies prior to our appearance at the hotel. I think it right for me to clear the slate, Ransom. Who knows what we may wish to write upon it next?"

A slight shiver on Ransom's part was the sole answer he gave to this innuendo; then both settled themselves to work, the eyes of either flashing hither and thither from one small object to another, in this seemingly deserted room. In the momentary silence which followed, the even breathing of the woman in the adjoining room could be distinctly heard. It seemed to affect Mr. Ransom deeply, though he strove hard to maintain the business-like attitude he had assumed from the beginning of this unofficial examination.

"She has confided nothing more to you since your return from the river bank?" suggested the lawyer.

"No."

The word came sharply, considering Mr. Ransom's usual manner. The lawyer showed surprise but no resentment, and turned his attention to the bag both had noted lying open on two chairs.

"Nothing equivocal here," he declared, after a moment's careful scrutiny of its remaining contents. "The only comment I should make in regard to what I find here is that all the articles are less carefully chosen than you would expect from one of your wife's fondness for fine appointments."

"They were collected in a hurry and possibly by telephone," returned the unhappy husband, after a shrinking glance into the bag. "The ones she provided in anticipation of her wedding are at the hotel in New York. In the trunks and bags there you will find articles as elegant as you could wish." Here he turned to the dresser, and pointed to the various objects grouped upon it.

"These show that she arranged herself with care for her meeting with you last night. How did she appear at that interview? Natural?"

"Hardly; she was much too excited. But I had no suspicion of what she was cherishing in her mind. I thought her intentions whimsical, and endeavored to edge in a little advice, but she was in no mood to receive it. Her mind was too full of what she intended to do.

"Here's where she ate her supper," he added, picking up a morsel of crust from a table set against the wall. "And so this door was found fastened on this side?" he proceeded, laying his hand on the broken lock.

"It had to be burst open, you see."

"And the window?"

"Was up. The carpet, as you can tell by look and feeling, is still wet with the soaking it got."

Mr. Harper's air changed to one of reluctant conviction.

"The evidence seems conclusive of your wife having left this room and the house in the remarkable manner stated by Miss Hazen. Yet—"

This yet showed that he was not as thoroughly convinced as the first phrase would show. But he added nothing to it; only stood listening, apparently to the even breathing of the sleeper on the other side of this loosely hanging door.

As he did so, his eye encountered the hot, dry gaze of Mr. Ransom, fixed upon him in a suspense too cruel to prolong, and with a sudden change of manner he moved from the door, saying significantly as he led the way out:

"Let us have a word or two in your own room. It is a principle of mine not to trust even the ears of the deaf with what it is desirable to keep secret."

Had the glance with which he said this lingered a moment longer on his companion's face, he would undoubtedly have been startled at the effect of his own words. But being at heart a compassionate man, or possibly understanding his new client much better than that client supposed, he had turned quite away in crossing the threshold, and so missed the conscious flash which for a moment replaced the somber and feverish expression that had already aged by ten years the formerly open features of this deeply grieved man.

Once in the hall, it was too dark to note further niceties of expression, and by the time Mr. Ransom's room was reached, purpose and purpose only remained visible in either face.

As they were crossing the threshold, the lawyer wheeled about and cast a quick look behind him.

"I observe," said he, "that you have a full and unobstructed view from here of the whole hall and of the two doors where our interest is centered. I presume you kept a strict watch on both last night. You let nothing escape you?"

"Nothing that one could see from this room."

With a thoughtful air, the lawyer swung to the door behind them. As it latched, the face of Mr. Ransom sharpened. He even put out a hand and rested it on a table standing near, as if to support himself in anticipation of what the lawyer would say now that they were again closeted together.

Mr. Harper was not without his reasons for a corresponding agitation, but he naturally controlled himself better, and it was with almost a judicial air that he made this long-expected but long-deferred suggestion:

"You had better tell me now, and as explicitly as possible, just what is in your mind. It will prevent all misunderstanding between us, as well as any injudicious move on my part."

Mr. Ransom hesitated, leaning hard on the table; then, with a sudden burst, he exclaimed:

"It sounds like folly, and you may think that my troubles have driven me mad. But I have a feeling here— a feeling without any reason or proof to back it—that the woman now sleeping off her exhaustion in Anitra's room is the woman I courted and married—Georgian Hazen, now Georgian Ransom, my wife."

"Good! I have made no mistake. That is my thought, too," responded the lawyer.

CHAPTER XV

ANITRA

A few minutes later they were discussing this amazing possibility.

"I have no reason for this conclusion,—this hope," admitted Mr. Ransom. "It is instinct with me, an intuition, and not the result of my judgment. It came to me when she first addressed me down by the mill-stream. If you consider me either wrong or misled, I confess that I shall not be able to combat your decision with any argument plausible enough to hold your attention for a moment."

"But I don't consider you either wrong or misled," protested the other. "That is," he warily added, "I am ready to accept the correctness of the possibility you mention and afterwards to note where the supposition will lead us. Of course, your first sensation is that of relief."

"It will be when I am no longer the prey of doubts."

"Notwithstanding the mystery?"

"Notwithstanding the mystery. The one thing I have found it impossible to contemplate is her death;— the extinction of all hope which death alone can bring. She has become so blended with my every thought since the hour she vanished from my eyes and consequently from my protection, that I should lose the better part of my self in losing her. Anything but that, Mr. Harper."

"Even possible shame?"

"How, shame?"

"Some reason very strong and very vital must underlie her conduct if what we suspect is true, and she has not only been willing to subject you and herself to a seeming separation by death, but to burden herself with the additional misery of being obliged to assume a personality cumbered by such a drawback to happiness and even common social intercourse as this of the supposed Anitra."

"You mean her deafness?"

"I mean that, yes. What could Mrs. Ransom's motive be (if the woman sleeping yonder is Mrs. Ransom) for so tremendous a sacrifice as this you ascribe to her? The rescue of her sister from some impending calamity? That would argue a love of long standing and of superhuman force; one far transcending even her natural affection for the husband to whom she has just given her hand. Such a love under such circumstances is not possible. She has known this long-lost sister for a few days only. Her sense of duty towards her, even her compassion for one so unfortunate, might lead her to risk much, but not so much as that. You must look for some other explanation; one more reasonable and much more personal."

"Where? where? I'm all at sea; blinded, dazed, almost at my wits' end. I can see no reason for anything she has done. I neither understand her nor understand myself. I ought to shrink from the poor creature there, sleeping off—I don't know what. But I don't. I feel drawn to her, instead, irresistibly drawn, as if my place were at her bedside to comfort and protect."

At this impulsive assertion springing from a depth of feeling for which the staid lawyer had no measure, a perplexed frown chased all the urbanity from his face. Some thought, not altogether welcome, had come to disturb him. He eyed Mr. Ransom closely from under his clouded brows. He could do this now with impunity, for Mr. Ransom's glances were turned whither his thoughts and inclinations had wandered.

"I would advise you," came in slow comment from the watchful lawyer, "not to be too certain of your conclusions till doubt becomes an absolute impossibility. Instinct is a good thing but it must never be regarded as infallible. It may be proved that it is your wife who has fled, after all. In which case it would be a great mistake to put any faith in this gipsy girl, Anitra."

Mr. Ransom's face hardened; his eyes did not leave the direction in which they were set.

"I will remember," said he.

His companion did not appear satisfied, and continued emphatically:

"Whether the woman now here is Mrs. Ransom or her wild and irresponsible sister, she is a person of dangerous will and one not to be lightly regarded nor carelessly dealt with. Pray consider this, Mr. Ransom, and do not allow impulse to supersede judgment. If you will take my advice—"

"Speak."

"I should treat her as if she were the woman she calls herself, or, at least, as if you thought her so. Nothing—" this word he repeated as he noted the incredulity with which the other listened—"would be so likely to make her betray herself as that."

"Let us go back and listen again at her door," was Mr. Ransom's emphatic but inconsequent reply.

The lawyer desisted from further advice, but sighed as he followed his new client into the hall. At the turn of the staircase they were stopped by the sound of wrangling voices in the office below. Mr. Harper heard his name mentioned and hastened to interfere. Assuring Mr. Ransom of his speedy return, he stepped down-stairs, and in a few minutes reappeared with a middle-aged man of characteristic appearance, whom he introduced to Mr. Ransom as Mr. Goodenough. The sight of the uncouth head of their youthful acquaintance of the morning peering up after him from the foot of the stairs was warranty sufficient that this was the man who had met the strange young lady on the highway early that morning.

At sight of him Mr. Ransom felt that inner recoil which we all experience at the prospect of an immediate and definite termination of a long brooding doubt. In another instant and with one word this uncultured and hitherto unknown man would settle for him the greatest question of his life. And he did not feel prepared for it. He had an impulse almost of flight, as if in this way he could escape a certainty he feared. What certainty? Perhaps he could not have answered had he been asked. His mind was in a turmoil. He had feelings—instincts; that was all.

The lawyer, noting his condition, undertook the leadership of affairs. Beckoning Mr. Goodenough into Mr. Ransom's room, he softly closed the door upon the many inquiring ears about, and, assuming the manner most likely to encourage the unsophisticated but straightforward looking man with whom he had to deal, quietly observed:

"We hear that you met this morning a young girl going towards the Ferry. There is great reason why we should know just how this young girl looks. A lady disappeared from here last night, and though, from a letter she left behind her, we have every reason to believe that her body is somewhere in the river, yet we don't want to overlook the possibility of her having escaped alive in another direction. Can you describe the person you saw?"

"Wa'al, I'm not much good at talk," was the embarrassed, almost halting reply. "I saw the gal and I remember just how she looked, but I couldn't put it into words to save my soul. She was pretty and chipper and walked along as if she was part of the mornin'; but that don't tell you much, does it? Yet I don't know what else to say. P'raps you could help me by asking questions."

"We'll see. Was she light-complexioned? Yellow hair, you know, and blue eyes?"

"No; I don't think she was. Not what I call light. My Sal's light; this gal wasn't like my Sal."

"Dark, then, very dark, with a gipsy color and snapping black eyes?"

"No, not that either. What I should call betweens. But more dark than light."

Harper flashed a glance at Ransom before putting his next question.

"What did she have on her head?"

"Bless me if I can tell! It wasn't a sun-bonnet, nor was it slapped all over with ribbons and flowers like my darter's."

"But she had some sort of hat on?"

"Sartain. Did you think she was just running to the neighbors?"

"But she wore no coat?"

"I don't remember any coat."

"Do you remember her frock?"

"No, not exactly."

"Don't you remember its color?"

"No."

"Wasn't it black? the skirt of it, at least?"

"Black? Wa'al, I guess not. A gal of her age in black! No, she was as bright as the flowers in my wife's garden. Not a black thing on her. I should sooner think her clothes were red than black."

Harper showed his surprise.

"Not a black skirt?" he persisted.

"No, sir'ee. I haven't much eye for fixin's but I've eye enough to know when a gal's dressed like a gal and not like some old woman."

Harper's eye stole again towards Ransom.

"Checkmate in four moves," he muttered. "The person we are interested in could have worn no such clothing as Mr. Goodenough describes. Yet clothing can be changed. How, I cannot see in this instance; but I will risk no mistake. The trail we followed led too surely in the direction of the highway for us to drop all inquiries because of a colored skirt and a hat we cannot quite account for. If the face is one we know (and I really believe it was), we can leave the other discrepancies to future explanation." And turning back to the patient countryman, he composedly remarked: "You are positive in your recollections of the young lady's features. You would have no difficulty in recognizing her if you saw her again?"

"Not a bit. Once I get a picter in my mind of a man or a woman I see it always. And I can see her as plain as plain the moment I stop to think. She was pretty, you see, and just a little scared to speak to a stranger. But that went as she saw my face, and she asked me very perlite if she was on the right road to the Ferry."

"And you told her she was?"

"Sartain; and how much time she had to get there to catch the boat."

"I see. So you would know her again if you saw her."

"I jest would."

The lawyer made a move towards the door which Mr. Ransom hastened to open. As the long vista of the hall disclosed itself, Mr. Harper turned upon the countryman with the quiet remark:

"There were two ladies here, you know. Twins. Their likeness was remarkable. If we show you the remaining one who now lies asleep, you surely will be able to tell if she is like the lady you saw."

"If she looks just like her you can bet beans against potatoes on that."

"Come, then. You needn't feel any embarrassment, for she's not only sound asleep but so deaf she couldn't hear you if she were awake. You need only take one glance and nod your head if she looks like the other. It is very desirable that none of us should speak. The case is a mysterious one and there's enough talk about it already without the women hiding and listening behind every shut door you see, adding their gossip to the rest."

A knowing look, a twitch at the corners of a good-natured mouth, and the man followed them down the hall, past one or two of the doors alluded to, till they reached the one against the panel of which Mr. Ransom had already laid his ear.

"Still asleep," his gesture seemed to signify; and with a word of caution he led the way in.

The room was very dark. Mrs. Deo had been careful to draw down the shade when she put her strange charge to bed, and at this first moment of entrance it was impossible for them to see more than the outline of a dark head upon a snowy pillow. But gradually, feature by feature of the sleeping woman's countenance became visible, and the lawyer, turning his acute gaze on the man from whose recognition he expected so much, impatiently awaited the nod which was to settle their doubt.

But that nod did not come, not even after Mr. Ransom, astonished at the long pause, turned on the stranger his own haggard and inquiring eyes. Instead, Mr. Goodenough lifted a blank stare to either face beside him, and, shaking his head, stumbled awkwardly back in an endeavor to leave the room. Mr. Ransom, taken wholly by surprise, uttered some peremptory ejaculation, but a glance from the lawyer quieted him, and not till they were all shut up again in that convenient room at the head of the stairs did any of the three speak.

And not even then without an embarrassed pause. Both the lawyer and his unhappy client had a deep and, in the case of the latter, a heartrending disappointment to overcome, and the clock on the stairs ticked out several seconds before the lawyer ventured to remark:

"Miss Hazen's face is quite new to you, I perceive. Evidently it was not her twin sister you met on the high road this morning."

"Nor anything like her," protested the man. "A different face entirely; prettier and more saucy. Such a gal as a man like me would be glad to call darter."

"Oh, I see!" assented the lawyer. Then with the instinctive caution of his class, "You have made no mistake?"

"Not a bit of a one," emphasized the other. "Sorry I can't give the gentleman any hope, but if the sisters look alike, it was not this woman's twin I met. I'm ready to take my oath on that."

"Very well. One catches at straws in a stress like this. Here's a fiver to pay for your trouble, and another for the lad who brought you here. Good day. We had no sound reason for expecting any different result from our experiment."

The man bowed awkwardly and went out. Mr. Harper brought down his fist heavily on the table, and after a short interval of silence, during which he studiously avoided meeting his companion's eye, he remarked:

"I am as much taken aback as yourself. For all he had to say about her gay clothing, I expected a different result. The girl on the highway was neither Mrs. Ransom nor her sister. We have made a confounded mistake and Mrs. Ransom—"

"Don't say it. I'm going back to the room where that woman lies sleeping. I cannot yet believe that my heart is not shut up within its walls. I'm going to watch for her eyes to open. Their expression will tell me what I want to know;—the look one gives before full realization comes and the soul is bare without any thought of subterfuge."

"Very well. I should probably do the same if I were you. Only your insight may be affected by prejudice. You will excuse me if I join you in this watch. The experiment is of too important a character for its results to depend upon the correct seeing of one pair of eyes."

CHAPTER XVI

"LOVE!"

She lay in the abandonment of profound slumber, one hand under her cheek, the other hidden by the white spread Mrs. Deo had been careful to draw closely about her. Both Mr. Harper and Mr. Ransom regretted this fact, for each instinctively felt that in her hands, if not in her sleeping face, they should be able to read the story of her life. If that life had been a hard one, such as must have befallen the waif, Anitra, her hands should show it.

But her hands were covered. And so, or nearly so, was her face; the latter by her long and curling locks of whose beauty I have hitherto spoken. One cheek only was visible, and this cheek looked dark to Ransom, decidedly darker than Georgian's; but realizing that the room itself was dark, he forbore to draw the attention of the lawyer to it, or even to allow it to affect his own judgment to the extent it reasonably called for.

His first scrutiny over, Mr. Harper crossed over to his old seat against the wall. Mr. Ransom remained by the bed. And thus began their watch.

It was a long and solemn one; a tedious waiting. The gloom and quiet of the small room was so profound that both men, for all their suspense and absorption in the event they awaited, welcomed the sound of a passing whisper or the careful stepping of feet in the corridor without.

If they turned to look they could just catch the outline of each other's countenance, but this they did not often attempt. Their attention was held by the silent figure on the bed, and so motionless was this figure in the profound slumber in which it lay enchained, and so motionless were they in their increasing suspense and expectation, that time seemed to have come to a standstill in this little room. There was one break. The lips which had hitherto remained mute opened in a quiet murmur, and Mr. Harper, watching his client, saw him clutch the headboard in sudden emotion before he finally rose and, with looks still fixed on the bed, approached him with the startling announcement:

"The word she whispered was 'Love'! It must be Georgian."

Alas! the same thought struck them both. Was this a proof? Mr. Ransom flushed hotly and crept softly back to his post.

Again time seemed to stop. Then there came a cautious rap on the door, followed by the hasty retreat of the person knocking. It caused Mr. Ransom to stir slightly, but did not affect the lawyer. Suddenly the former rose with every evidence of renewed agitation. This drew Mr. Harper from his seat.

"What is it?" he cried, softly approaching the other and whispering, though after events proved that he might have spoken aloud with impunity.

Mr. Ransom pointed to her temple from which her hair had just fallen away.

"The veining here. I have often studied it. I recognize its every convolution. It is Georgian, Georgian who lies there—ah, she's stirring, waking! Let me go—"

He dragged himself from Mr. Harper's detaining hand, bent over the bed and murmured softly but with the thrilling intensity of a suffering, hoping heart, the name which at that moment meant the whole wide world to him:

"Georgian!"

Would she greet this expression with recognition and a smile? The lawyer half expected her to and stepped near enough to see, but the eyes which had opened upon the white wall in front of her stared on, and when they did turn, as they did after one halting, agonizing minute, it was in response to some movement made by Mr. Ransom and not in reply to his voice.

This sudden and unexpected overthrow of his secretly cherished hopes was terrible. As he saw her rise on one elbow and meet his gaze with one which revealed the astonishment and resentment of a wild creature suddenly entrapped, he felt, or so he afterwards declared, as if the viper which had hitherto clung cold and deathlike about his heart had suddenly sprung to life and stung him. It was the most uncanny moment of his life.

Aghast at the effect of this upon his own mind, he reeled from the room, followed by the lawyer. As they passed down the hall they heard her voice raised to a scream in uncontrollable shame and indignation. This was followed by the snap of her key in the lock.

They had made a great mistake, or so the lawyer decided when they again stood face to face in Mr. Ransom's room. That the latter made no immediate answer was no proof that he did not coincide in the other's opinion. Indeed it was only too evident that he did, for his first words, when he had controlled himself sufficiently to speak, were these:

"I should have taken your advice. In future I will. To me she is henceforth Anitra, and I shall treat her as my wife's sister. Watch if I fail. Anitra! Anitra!" He reiterated the word as if he would fix it in his mind as well as accustom his lips to it. Then he wheeled about and faced Harper, whose eyes he doubtless felt on him. "Yet I am not so thoroughly convinced as to feel absolute peace here," he admitted, striking his breast with irrepressible passion. "My good sense tells me I am a fool, but my heart whispers that the sweetness in her sleeping face was the sweetness which won me to love Georgian Hazen. That gentle sweetness! Did you note it?"

"Yes, I noted what you mention. But don't let that influence you too much. The wildest heart has its tender moments, and her dreams may have been pleasant ones."

Mr. Ransom remembered her unconscious whisper and felt stunned, silenced. The lawyer gave no evidence of observing this, but remarked quite easily and with evident sincerity:

"I am more readily affected by proof than you are. I am quite convinced myself, that our wits have been wool-gathering. There was no mistaking her look of outraged womanhood. It was not your wife who encountered your look, but the deaf Anitra. Of course, you won't believe me. Yet I advise you to do so. It would be too dreadful to find that this woman really is your wife."

"What?"

"I know what I am saying. Nothing much worse could happen to you. Don't you see where the hypothesis to which you persist in clinging would land you? Should the woman in there prove to be your wife Georgian—" The lawyer stopped and, in a tone the seriousness of which could not fail to impress his agitated hearer, added quietly, "you remember what I said to you a short time ago about guilt."

"Guilt!"

"No, the word was shame. But guilt better expresses my meaning. I repeat, should the woman prove to be, not the lovely but ignorant girl she appears, but Georgian Ransom, your wife, then upon her must fall the onus of Anitra's disappearance if not of her possible death. No! you must hear me out; the time has come for plain speaking. Your wife had her reasons—we do not know what they were, but they were no common ones—for wishing this intrusive sister out of the way. Anitra, on the contrary, could have desired nothing so much as the preservation of her protector. The conclusion is not an agreeable one. Let us hope that the question it involves will never be presented for any man's consideration."

Mr. Ransom sank speechless into a chair. This last blow was an overwhelming one and he sank before it.

Mr. Harper altered his tone. He had real commiseration for his client and had provided himself with an antidote to the poison he had just so ruthlessly administered.

"Courage!" he cried. "I only wished you to see that there were worse losses to consider than that of your wife's desertion, even if that desertion took the form of suicide. There is a reason which you have forgotten for acquitting Mrs. Ransom of such criminal intentions and of accepting as your sister-in-law the woman who calls herself Anitra. Recall Mrs. Ransom's will; the general terms of which I felt myself justified in confiding to you. In it there are no provisions made for this Anitra. Had Mrs. Ransom, for any inexplicable reason, planned an exchange of identities with her sorely afflicted sister, she would have been careful to have left that sister some portion of her great fortune. But she did not remember her with a cent. This fact is very significant and should give you great comfort."

"It should, it should, in face of the other alternative you have suggested as possible. But I fear that I am past comfort. In whatever light we regard this tragedy, it all means woe and disaster to me. I have made a mess of my life and I have got to face the fact like a man." Then rising and confronting Mr. Harper with passionate intensity, he called out till the room rang again:

"Georgian is dead! You hear me, Georgian is dead!"

CHAPTER XVII

"I DON'T HEAR"

The afternoon passed without further developments. Mr. Harper, who had his own imperative engagements, left on the evening train for New York, promising to return the next day in case his presence seemed indispensable to his client.

That client's final word to him had been an injunction to keep an eye on Georgian's so-called brother and to report how he had been affected by the news from Sitford; and when, in the lull following the lawyer's departure, Mr. Ransom sat down in his room to look his own position resolutely in the face, this brother and his possible connection with the confusing and unhappy incidents of this last fatal week regained that prominent place in his thoughts which the doubts engendered by the unusual character of these incidents had for a while dispelled.

What had been the hold of this strange and uncongenial man on Georgian? And was his reappearance at the same time with that of a supposedly long deceased sister simply a coincidence so startling as to appear unreal?

He had not seen Anitra again and did not propose to, unless the meeting came about in a natural way and without any show of desire on his part. If any suspicion had been awakened in the house by his peculiar conduct in the morning, he meant it to be speedily dissipated by the careful way in which he now held to his rôle of despairing husband whose only interest in the girl left on his hands was the dutiful one of a reluctant brother-in-law, who doubts the kindly feelings of his strange and unwelcome charge.

The landlady, with a delicacy he highly appreciated, cared for the young girl without making her conspicuous by any undue attention. No tidings had come in of any discovery in the mill-stream or in the river into which it ran, and there being nothing with which to feed gossip, the townsfolk who had gathered about the hotel porches gradually began to disperse, till only a few of the most persistent remained to keep up conversation till midnight.

Finally these too left and the house sank into quiet, a quiet which remained unbroken all night; for everybody, even poor Mr. Ransom, slept.

He was up, however, with the first beam entering his room. How could he tell but that news of a definite and encouraging nature awaited him? Some one might have come in early from town or river. All search had not been abandoned. There were certain persistent ones who had gone as far as Beardsley's. Some of these might have returned. He would hasten down and see. But it was only to find the office empty, and though the household presently awoke and the great front door was thrown open to all comers, no eager straggler came rushing in with the tidings he equally longed and dreaded to receive.

At half-past ten the representative of the county police called on Mr. Ransom, but with small result. Shortly after his departure, the mail came in and with it the New York papers. These he read with avidity. But they added nothing to his knowledge. Georgian's death was accepted as a fact, and the peculiarities of their history since their unfortunate wedding-day were laid bare with but little consideration for his feelings or the good name of his bride. With a sorer heart than ever, he flung the papers from him and went out to gather strength in the open air.

There was a corner of the veranda into which he had never ventured. It was likely to be a solitary one at this hour, and thither he now went. But a shock awaited him there. A lady was pacing its still damp boards. A lady who did not turn her head at his step, but whom he instantly recognized from her dress, and wilful but not ungraceful bearing, as her whom he was determined to call, nay recognize, as Anitra Hazen.

His judgment counseled retreat, but the fascination of her presence held him, and in that moment of hesitation she turned towards him and flight became impossible.

It was the first opportunity he had had of observing her features in broad daylight. The effect was a confused one. She was Georgian and she was not Georgian. Her skin was decidedly darker, her eyes more lustrous, her bearing less polished and at the same time more impassioned. She was not so tall or quite so elegantly proportioned;—or was it her rude method of dressing her hair and the awkward cut of her clothes which made the difference. He could not be sure. Resolved as he was to consider her Anitra, and excellent as his reasons were for doing so, the swelling of his heart as he met her eye roused again the old doubt and gave an unnatural tone to his voice as he advanced towards her with an impetuous utterance of her name:

"Anitra!"

She shrunk, not at the word but at his movement, which undoubtedly was abrupt; but immediately recovered herself and, meeting him half-way, cried out in the unnaturally loud tones of the very deaf:

"They don't bring my sister back. She is drowned, drowned. But you still have Anitra," she exclaimed in child-like triumph. "Anitra will be good to you. Don't forsake the poor girl. She will go where you go and be very obedient and not get angry ever again."

He felt his hair rise. Something in her look, something in her manner of making evident the indefinable barrier between them even while expressing her desire to accompany him, made such a disturbance in his brain that for the moment he no longer knew himself, nor her, nor the condition of things about him. If she saw the effect she produced, she gave no evidence of it. She had begun to smile and her smile transformed her. The wild look which was never long out of her eyes softened into a milder gleam, and dimples he had been accustomed to see around lips he had kissed and called the sweetest in the world flashed for a moment in the face before him with a story of love he dared not read, yet found it impossible to forget or see unmoved.

"What trial is this into which my unhappy fate has plunged me!" thought he. "Can reason stand it? Can I see this woman daily, hourly, and not go mad between my doubts and my love?"

His face had turned so stern that even she noticed it, and in a trice the offending dimples disappeared.

"You are angry," she pouted. "You don't want Anitra. Nod if it is so, nod and I will go away."

He did not nod; he could not. She seemed to gather courage at this, and though she did not smile again, she gave him a happy look as she said:

"I have no home now, nor any friend since sister has gone. I don't want any if I can stay with you and learn things. I want to be like sister. She was nice and wore pretty clothes. She gave me some, but I don't know where they are. I don't like this dress. It's black and all bad round the bottom where I fell into the mud."

She looked down at her dress. It showed, in spite of Mrs. Deo's effort at cleaning it, signs of her tramp through the wet lane. He looked at it too, but it was mechanically. He was debating in his mind a formidable question. Should he grasp her hand, insist that she was Georgian and demand her confidence and the truth? or should he follow the lawyer's advice and continue to accept appearances, meet her on her own ground and give her the answer called for by her lonely and forsaken position? He found after a moment's thought that he had no choice; that he could not do the first and must do the last.

"You shall come with me," said he quietly. "I will see that you have every suitable protection and care."

She surveyed him with the same unmoved inquiry burning in her eyes.

"I don't hear," said she.

He looked at her, his lips set, his eyes as inquiring as her own.

"I don't believe it," he muttered just above his breath.

The steady stare of her eyes never faltered.

"You loved sister, love me," she whispered.

He fell back from her. This was not Georgian. This was the untutored girl about whom Georgian had written to him. Everything proved it, even her hands upon which his eyes now fell. Why had he not noticed them before? He had meant to look at them the first thing. Now that he did, he saw that he might have spared himself some of the miserable uncertainties of the last few minutes. They were small and slight like Georgian's, but very brown and only half cared for. That they were cared for at all astonished him. But she soon explained that. Seeing where his eyes were fixed, she cried out:

"Don't look at my hands. I know they are not real nice like sister's. But I'm learning. She showed me how to rub them white and cut the nails. A woman did it for me the first time and I've been doing it ever since, but they don't look like hers, for all the pretty rings she bought me. Was I foolish to want the rings? I always had rings when I was with the gipsies. They were not gold ones, but I liked them. And Mother Duda liked rings too and made me one once out of beads. It was on my finger when my sister took me home with her. That is why she brought me these. She didn't think the bead one was good enough. It wasn't much like hers."

Ransom recalled the diamonds and the rich sapphires he had been accustomed to see on his bride's hand.

But this did not engage him long. Some method of communication must be found with this girl, which could be both definite and unmistakable. Feeling in his pocket, he brought out pencil and a small pad. He would write what he had to say, and was hesitating over the words with which to open this communication, when he saw her hand thrust itself between his eyes and the pad, and heard these words uttered in a resolute tone, but not without a hint of sadness:

"I cannot read. I have never been taught."

PART III

MONEY

CHAPTER XVIII

GOD'S FOREST, THEN MAN'S

The pencil and pad fell from Mr. Ransom's hands. He stared at the girl who had made this astonishing statement, and his brain whirled.

As for her, she simply stooped and picked up the pad.

"You feel badly about that," said she. "You want me to read. I'll learn. That will make me more like sister. But I know some things now. I know what you are thinking about. You are curious about my life, what it has been and what kind of a girl I am. I'll tell you. I can talk if I cannot hear. I heard up to two years ago. Shall I talk now? Shall I tell you what I told Georgian when she found me crying in the street and took me home to her house?"

He nodded blindly.

With a smile as beautiful as Georgian's—for a moment he thought more beautiful—she drew him to a seat. She was all fire and purpose now. The spark of intelligence which was not always visible in her eye burned brightly. She would have looked lovely even to a stranger, but he was not thinking of her looks, only of the hopelessness of the situation, its difficulties and possibly its perils.

"I don't remember all that has happened to me," she began, speaking very fast. "I never tried to remember, when I was little; I just lived, and ran wild in the roads and woods like the weasels and the chipmunks. The gipsies were good to me. I had not a cross word in years. The wife of the king was my friend, and all I knew I learned from her. It was not much, but it helped me to live in the forest and be happy, as long as I was a little girl. When I grew up it was different. It was the king who was kind then, and the woman who was fierce. I didn't like his kindness, but she didn't know this, for after one day when she caught him staring at me across the fire, she sent me off after something she wanted in a small town we were camping near, and when I came back with it, the band was gone. I tried to follow, but it was dark and I didn't know the way; besides I was afraid—afraid of him. So I crept back to the town and slept in the straw of a barn I found open. Next day I sold my earrings and got bread. It didn't last long and I tried to work, but that meant sleeping under a roof, and houses smothered me, so I did my work badly and was turned out. Then I sold my ring. It was my last trinket, and when the few cents I got for it were gone, I wandered about hungry. This I was used to and didn't mind at first, but at last I went to work again, and I did better now for a little while, till one evening I saw, through the stable window of the inn where I was working, two black eyes staring in just as they stared across the dying embers of the gipsy camp. I did not scream, but I hid myself, and when they were gone away stole out and got on the cars, and gave the man my last dollar—all the money I had earned—for a ride to New York. I did not know any better. I knew he never went to New York, and I thought I would be safe from him there. But of the difference between the woods and a forest of brick and stone I never thought; of night with no shelter but the wall of some blind alley; of hunger in the sight of food, and wild beasts in the shape of men. I didn't know where to go or who to speak to. If any one stared at me long, I turned and ran away. I ran away once from a policeman. He thought me a thief, and started to run after me. But people slipped in between us and I got away. What happened next I don't know. Perhaps I was thrown down, perhaps I fell. I had come a long way and I was tired. When I did know anything, I was lying on my back in a narrow street, looking up at a tall building that seemed to go right up into the sky like the great rocks I had sometimes slept under when I was with the gipsies. Only there were windows in the rock, out of which looked faces, and I got looking back at one of these faces and the face looked at me, and I liked it and got up on my knees and held up my arms, and the face drew back out of sight, and I felt very sorry and cried and almost laid down again. I seemed so alone and hurt and hungry. But the children—there were crowds of children—wouldn't let me. They got in a ring and pulled at me, and some one cried: 'Big cheeks is coming! Big cheeks will eat her up,' and I was angry and got up on my feet. But I couldn't walk; I screamed when I tried to, which frightened the children, and they all ran away. But I didn't fall; an arm was round me, a good, kind arm, and though I didn't see the face of the woman who helped, for she had her head wrapped up in an old shawl, I felt that it was the same which had looked out of the window at me, and went willingly enough when she began to draw me toward the house and up the first flight of stairs, though I could hardly help screaming every time my foot touched the ground. At the top of the first flight I stopped; I could go no further. The woman heard me pant, and pushing the covering from her eyes, she turned my face towards the light and looked at it. I thought she wanted to see if I was strong enough to go on, but that wasn't it at all, for in a minute I heard her say, in a voice so sweet I thought I had never heard the like, 'Yes, you're pretty; I want a pretty girl to stay with me and go about selling my things. I love pretty girls; I never was pretty myself. Will you stay with me if I take you up to my room and take care of you? I'll be good to you, little duckling, everybody about here will tell you that; everybody but the children, they don't like me.' I moaned, but it was from happiness. It seemed too good to hear that cooing voice in my ear. I thought of my mother—a dream—and my arms went up as they had in the street below. 'I will stay,' I said. She caught my hands and that is all I remember till I found myself in bed, with my ankle bound up and a gentle hand smoothing my hair. It was a month before I walked again. All the time this woman tended me, but always from behind. I did not see her face—not well—only by glimpses and then only partly, for the shawl was always over her head, covering everything but her eyes and mouth. These were small, the smallest I ever saw, little pig eyes, and little screwed up mouth; but the look of them was kindly and that was all I cared about then; that and her talk, which made me cry one minute and laugh the next. I have never cried so much or laughed so much in my life as I did that one month. She told such sad things and she told such funny ones. She made me glad to see her come in and sorry to see her go out. She let no one else come near me. I did not care; I liked her too well. I was never tired of listening to her praises and she praised me a great deal. I even did not mind sleeping under a roof as much as I had before, perhaps because we were so near it; perhaps because the room was so full of all sorts of things, I never got tired of looking at them. Pretty she called them, but when I saw more things, things outside in shop windows and the houses I afterwards went into, I knew they were very cheap things and not always pretty. But she thought they were, and used to talk about them by the hour and tell me stories she had made up about the pictures she had cut out of newspapers. And I learned something; I could not help it, and even began to think a bit—something I had never done before. But when I got on my feet again, and was given the choice of staying there all the time, I did not know at first whether I wanted to or not. For Mother Duda had been very honest with me, and the minute she found that I could walk again had told me that I would have to have great patience if I lived with her, and endure a very disagreeable sight. Then she pulled off her shawl and I saw her as she was and almost screamed, she looked so horrid to me, but I didn't quite, for her eyes wouldn't let me. They seemed to ask me not to care, but to love her a little though she was a fright to look at, and I tried but I couldn't, I could only keep from screaming.

"She had a goitre; that is what she called it, and the great pocket of flesh hanging down on either side of her neck frightened me. It frightened everybody; she was used to that, but she said she loved me and felt my fear more than she did others. Could I bear to live with her, knowing what her shawl hid? If I could she would be good to me, but if I couldn't she would do what she could to get me honest work in some other place. I didn't answer at first, but I did before she had put her shawl on again. I told her that

I would forget everything but her good smile, and stay with her a little while. I stayed three years, helping her by going about and selling the tatting work she made.

"She could make beautiful patterns and so neat, but she couldn't sell them, on account of her awful appearance. So I was very useful to her, and felt I was earning my meat and drink and the kind looks and words which made them taste good. It taught me a lot, going around. I saw people and how they lived and what was nice and what wasn't. I was only sorry that Mother Duda couldn't go too. She loved pretty things so. But she never went out except at a very early hour in the morning, so early that it was still dark. It seemed a terrible hour to me, but she always came in with a smile, and when one day I asked her why, she said, because she saw so many other poor creatures out at this same hour, who were worse to look at than she was. This didn't seem possible to me, and once I went out with her to see. But I never went again. Such faces as we met; such deformity—men who never showed themselves by day—women who loved beauty and were hideous. We saw them on street corners—coming up cellar steps, slinking in and out of blind alleys—never where it was light—and they shrank from each other, but not from the policeman. They were not afraid of his eye; they were used to him and he to them. After I had passed a dozen such miserable creatures, I felt myself one of them and never wanted to go out at this hour again.

"Don't you believe this part of my story," she suddenly asked, looking up into Mr. Ransom's troubled face? "Ask the policeman who tramps about those streets every night; he'll tell you."

The question on Ransom's lips died. What use of asking what she could not hear.

"I wish I knew what you were thinking," she now murmured softly, so softly that he hardly caught the words. "But I never shall, I never shall. I will tell you now how I became deaf," she promised after a moment of wistful gazing. "Is there any one near? Can anybody hear me?" she continued, with a suspicious look about her.

He shook his head. It was the first movement he had made since she began her story.

This apparently reassured her, for she proceeded at once to say:

"Mother Duda had never told me anything about herself. It scared me then when one morning I found sitting at the breakfast table a man who she said was her son. He was big and pale looking, and had a slight swelling on one side of his neck which made me sick; but I tried to be polite, though I did not like him at all and had a sudden feeling of having no home any more. That was the first day. The next two were worse. For he didn't hate me as I did him, and wouldn't leave the house while I was there, saying he could not bear to be away from his mother. But he skipped out quick enough after I was gone, so the neighbors said, and sometimes I think he followed me. Mother Duda wasn't like her old self at all. She loved him, he was her son, but she didn't like all he did. She wanted him to work; he wouldn't work. He sat and stared at me as the gipsy king used to stare, and if I grew red and hot it was from shame and fear and horror of the great throat I saw growing from day to day, and which would some time be like his mother's. He knew I didn't like him, but he wasn't good like Mother Duda, and told me one day that he was going to make me his wife, whether I wanted him to or not, and talked about a great secret, and the big man he would be some day. This made me angry, and I said that all the bigness he would ever have would be in his neck. At which he struck me, right across the ear, hard, so hard that I fell on the floor with a scream, and Mother Duda came running. He was sorry then and threw down the thing he had in his hand; but the harm had been done and I was sick a month and had doctors and awful pain, and when I was well again I couldn't hear a sound with that ear. Hans wasn't there while I was ill; I shouldn't have got well if he had been; but he came back when I was up again and was very meek though he didn't stop looking at me. I thought I would run away one day, and went out without my basket, but after I had tried two whole days to get work and couldn't, I went back. Mother Duda almost squeezed the heart out of me for joy, and Hans went down on his knees and promised not to do or say anything more that I didn't like. He even promised to go to work, but his work was of a queer kind. It kept him in his little room and meant spending money, and not getting it. Men came to see him and were locked up with him in his little room. And if he went out, he locked the door and took the key away, and said great times were coming and that I would be glad to marry him some day, whether his neck was big or small. But I knew I shouldn't and kept very close to Mother Duda and begged her to get me a new home, and she promised and I was feeling happier, when one day Hans was called out by a man and went away so fast that he forgot to lock his door, and Mother Duda and I went into the room, and it was then that the thing happened which spoiled all my life. I don't understand it. I never did, for no one could tell me anything after that day. Mother Duda had gone up to a table and was moving things about, trying to see what they were, when everything turned black, the room shook, and I was whirling all about, trying to take hold of things which seemed to be falling about me, till I too fell. When I knew anything, there was lots of people looking at me; people of the house, men, women, and children, but what was strangest of all was the awful stillness. No one made any sound—nothing made any sound, though I saw an old book-shelf tumble down from the wall while I was looking, and people moved about and opened their lips and seemed to be talking. Had Hans struck me again? I began to think so, and got up from the floor where I was lying and tried to call out, but my voice made no noise though people looked around as if it had, and I felt an awful fright, not only for myself but for Mother Duda, who was being carried out of the door by two men, and who did not move at all and who never moved again. Poor Mother Duda, she was killed and I was deaf. I knew it after a little while, but I don't know what did it; something that Hans had; something that Mother Duda touched—a square something—I had just caught a glimpse of it in Mother Duda's hand when the room flew into a wreck and I became what I am now."

"Dynamite," murmured Ransom; then paused and had a small struggle with his heart, for she was looking up into his face, demanding sympathy with Georgian's eyes; and being close together on the short seat, he could not help but feel her shudders and share the intense excitement which choked her.

"Oh," she cried, as he laid his hand a moment on her arm and then took it away again, "one minute to hear! the next to find the world all still, always still,—a poor girl—not knowing how to read or write! But you cannot care about that; you cannot care about me. It's sister you want to hear about, how she came to find me; how we came here for new and terrible things to happen; always for new and terrible things to happen which I don't understand.

"Hans never came back. All sorts of policemen came into the house, doctors came, priests came, but no Hans. Mother Duda was buried, I rode in a coach at the funeral, but still no Hans. The old life was over, and when the food was all gone from the shelves, I took my little basket and went out, not meaning to come back again. And I did not. I sold my basket out; got a handful of pennies and went to the market to get something to eat. Then I went into a park, where there were benches, and sat down to rest. I did not know of any place to go to and began to cry, when a lady stopped before me, and I looked up and saw myself.

"I thought I was dreaming or had the fever again, as when I was sick with my ear, and I thought it was myself as I would look in heaven, for she had such beautiful clothes on and looked so happy. But when she talked, I could see her lips move and I couldn't hear; and I knew that I was just in the park with my empty basket and my onion and bread, and that the lady was a lady and no one I knew, only so like what I had seen of myself in the glass that I was shaking all over, and she was shaking all over, and neither of us could look away. And still her lips moved, and seeing her at last look frightened and angry that I didn't answer, I spoke and said that I was deaf; that I was very sorry that I couldn't hear because we looked so much alike, though she was a great lady and I was a very, very poor girl who hadn't any home or any friends, or anything to wear or eat but what she saw. At this her eyes grew bigger even than before, and she tried to talk some more, and when I shook my head she took hold of my arm and began drawing me away, and I went and we got on the cars, and she took me to a house and into a room where she took away my basket and put me in a chair, and took off first her hat, then my own, and showed me the two heads in a glass, and then looked at me so hard that I cried out, 'Sister,' which made her jump up and put her hand on her heart, then look at me again harder and harder, till I remembered way back in my life, and I said:

"'When I was a little girl I had a sister they called my twin. That was before I lived in the woods with the gipsies. Are you that sister grown up? The place where we played together had a tall fence with points at the top. There were flowers and there were bushes with currants on them all round the fence.'

"She made a sudden move, and I felt her arms about my neck. I think she cried a little. I didn't, I was too glad. I knew she was that sister the moment our faces touched, and I knew she would care for me, and that I needn't go back into the streets any more. So I kissed her and talked a good deal and told her what I've been telling, and she tried to answer, tried as you did to write, but all I could understand was that she meant to keep me, but not in the place where we were, and that I was to go out again. But she fixed me up a little before we went out, and she bought me some things, so that I looked different. Then we went into another house, where she talked with a woman for a long time, and then sat down with me and moved her lips very patiently, motioning me to watch and try to understand. But I was frightened and couldn't. So she gave up and, kissing me, made motions with her hands which I understood better; she wanted me to stay there while she went away, and I promised to if she would come back soon. At this she took out her watch. I was pleased with the watch, and she let me look at it, and inside against the cover I saw a picture. You know whose it was."

The depths to which her voice sank, the trembling of her tones, startled Ransom. Had she been less unfortunate, he would have moved to a different seat, but he could not show her a discourtesy after so pitiful a tale. But the nod he gave her was a grave one, and her cheek flushed and her head fell, as she softly added: "It was the first time I ever saw a face I liked—you won't mind my saying so,—and I wanted to keep the watch, but sister carried it away. She didn't tell me what it meant, her having your picture where she could see it all the time, but when she came again she made me know that you and she were married, by pointing at the picture and then throwing something white over her head; I didn't ask for the watch after that, but—"

A far-away look, a trembling of her whole body, finished this ingenuous confession. Ransom edged himself away and then was sorry for it, for her lip quivered and her hands, from being quiet, began that nervous interlacing of the fingers which bespeaks mental perturbation.

"I am very ignorant," she faltered; "perhaps I have said something wrong. I don't mean to, I want to be a good girl and please you, so that you won't send me away now sister is gone. Ah, I know what you want," she suddenly broke out, as he seized her by the arm and looked inquiringly at her. "You want me to tell why I jumped out of the carriage that night and vexed Georgian and was naughty and wouldn't speak to her. I can't, I can't. You wouldn't like it if I did. But I'm sorry now, and will never vex you, but do just what you want me to. Shall I go up-stairs now?"

He shook his head. How could he let her go with so much unsaid? She had talked frankly till she had reached the very place where his greatest interest lay. Then she had suddenly shown shyness of her subject and leaped the gap, as it were, to the present moment. How recall her to the hour when she had seen Georgian for the second time? How urge her into a description of those days succeeding his wife's flight from the hotel, of which he had no account, save the feverish lines of the letter she had sent him. He was racking his brain for some method of communicating his wishes to Anitra, when he heard steps behind him, and, turning, saw the clerk approaching him with a telegram.

He glanced at her slyly as he took it. Somehow he couldn't get used to her deafness, and expected her to give some evidence of surprise or curiosity. But she was still studying her hands, and as his eyes lingered on her downcast face he saw a tear well from her lids and wet the cheek she held partly turned from him. He wanted to kiss that tear, but refrained and opened his telegram instead. It was from Mr. Harper, and ran thus:

Expect a visitor. The man we know has left the St. Denis.

CHAPTER XIX

IN MRS. DEO'S ROOM

A prey to fresh agitation, he stepped back to Anitra's side. Surely she must understand that it was Georgian and not herself about whom he was most anxious to hear. But she did not seem to. The smile with which she greeted him suggested nothing of the past. It spoke only of the future.

"I will learn to be like sister," she impulsively cried out, rising and beaming brightly upon him. "I will forget the old gipsy ways and Mother Duda's ways, and try to be nice and pretty like my sister. And you shall learn me to read and write. I've known deaf people who learned. Then I shall know what you think; now I only know how you feel."

He shook his head, a little sadly, perhaps. There were people who could teach her these arts, but not he. He had neither the ability, the courage, nor the patience.

"Then some one shall learn me," she loudly insisted, her cheek flushing and her eye showing an angry spark. "I will not be ignorant always; I will not, I will not." And turning, she fled from his side, and he was left to think over her story and ask himself for the hundredth time what it all meant, what his own sensations meant, and what would be the outcome of conditions so complicated.

The possibly speedy appearance on the scene of Georgian's so-called brother did not detract from his difficulty. He felt helpless without the support of Mr. Harper's presence, and spent a very troubled forenoon listening to the mingled condolences and advice of people who had no interest in his concerns save such as sprang from curiosity and a morbid craving for excitement.

At two o'clock occurred the event of which he had been forewarned. A carriage drove up to the hotel and from it stepped two travelers; one of them a stranger, the other the man with the twisted jaw. Mr. Ransom advanced to meet the latter. He was anxious to listen to his first inquiries and, if possible, be the person to answer them.

He was successful in this. Mr. Hazen no sooner saw him than he accosted him without ceremony.

"What is this I hear and read about Georgian and her so-called twin?" he cried. "Nothing that I can believe, I want you to know. Georgian may have drowned herself. That is credible enough. But that the girl we read about in the papers and whom she evidently induced to come to this place with her should be the dead girl we called Anitra—why, that is all bosh—a tale to deceive the public, and possibly you, but not one to deceive me. The coincidence is much too improbable."

"'There are stranger things in heaven and earth'"—quoted Ransom; but Hazen was already in conversation with the group of hotel idlers who had crowded up at sound of his loud voice.

After a careful look which had taken in all of their faces, he had approached one young fellow, covering the lower part of his face as he did so.

"Halloo! Yates," he called out. "Don't you remember the day we tied two chickens together, leg to leg, and sent them tumbling down the hill back of old Wylie's barn?"

"Alf Hazen!" shouted the fellow, thus accosted. "Why, I thought you—"

"Dead, eh? Of course you did. So did everybody else. But I've come to life, you see. With sad marks of battle on me," he continued, dropping his hand. "You all recognize me?"

"Yes, yes," rose in one acclaim from a dozen or more throats after a moment of awkward uncertainty.

"I know the eyes," vigorously asserted one.

"And the voice," chimed in another. After which rose a confused babel of ejaculations and exclamatory questions, among which one could detect:

"How did it happen, Alf?" "What took off your jaw?" and other equally felicitous expressions.

"I'll tell you all about that later," he replied, after silence had in a measure been restored. "What I want to say now is this. Is it believable that simultaneously with my own return from the grave another member of my family should reappear before you from an older and much more certain burying? I tell you no. The riddle is one which calls for quite another solution and I have come to assist you in finding it."

Here he cast a sinister glance at Ransom.

The latter met the implied accusation with singular calmness.

"Any assistance will be welcome," said he, "which will enable us to solve this very serious problem." Then, as Hazen's lip curled, he added with dignified candor, "I scorn to retort by throwing any doubt on your assertion of relationship to my lost wife, or the possibility of these good people being misled by your confident bearing and a possible likeness about the eyes to the boy they knew. But one question I will hazard, and that before we have gone a step further. Why does it seem so credible to you that Georgian, a much loved and loving woman, should have leaped to a watery death within a week of her marriage? You have just stated that you found no difficulty in that. Does not that statement call for some explanation? All your old friends here must see that this is my due as well as hers."

For an instant the man hesitated, but in that instant his hand slipped from his mouth over which he had again laid it, and his whole face, with its changed lines and the threatening, almost cruel expression which these gave it, appeared in all its combined eagerness and force. A murmur escaped the watchful group about him, but this affected him little. His eyes, which he had fixed on Ransom, sharpened a trifle, perhaps, and his tone grew a thought more sarcastic as he finally retorted:

"I will explain myself to you but not to this crowd. And not to you till I am sure of the facts which as yet have reached me only through the newspapers. Let me hear a full account of what has transpired here since you all came to town. I have an enormous interest in the matter;—a family interest, as you are well aware for all your badly hidden insinuations."

"Follow me," was the quiet reply. "There is a room on this very floor where we can talk undisturbed."

Mr. Hazen cast a quick glance behind him at the man who had driven up with him and whom nobody had noticed till now. Then without a word he separated himself from the chattering group encircling him and stepped after Mr. Ransom into the small room where the latter had held his first memorable conversation with the lawyer.

"Now," said he as the door swung to behind them, "plain language and not too much of it. I have no time to waste, but the truth about Georgian I must know."

Ransom settled himself. He felt bound to comply with the other's request, but he wished to make sure of not saying too much, or too little. Hazen's attack had startled him. It revealed one of two things. Either this man of mystery had assumed the offensive to hide his own connection with this tragedy, or his antagonism was an honest one, springing from an utter disbelief in the circumstances reported to him by the press and such gossips as he had encountered on his way to Sitford.

With the first possibility he felt himself unable to cope without the aid of Mr. Harper; the second might be met with candor. Should he then be candid with this doubter, relate to him the facts as they had unrolled themselves before his own eyes;—secret facts—convincing ones—facts which must prove to him that whether Georgian did or did not lie at the bottom of the mill-stream, the woman now in the house was his sister Anitra, lost to him and the rest of the family for many years, but now found again and restored to her position as a Hazen and Georgian's twin. The discovery might not prove welcome. It would have a tendency to throw Mr. Hazen's own claim into the disrepute he would cast on hers. But this consideration could have no weight with Mr. Ransom. He decided upon candor at all costs. It suited his nature best, and it also suited the strange and doubtful situation. Mr. Harper might have concluded differently, but Mr. Harper was not there to give advice; and the matter would not wait. Little as he understood this Hazen, he recognized that he was not a man to trifle with. Something would have to be said or done.

Meeting the latter's eye frankly, he remarked:

"I have no wish to keep anything back from you. I am as much struck as you are by the mystery of this whole occurrence. I was as hard to convince. This is my story. It involves all that is known here with the exception of such facts as have been kept from us by the three parties directly concerned—of which three I consider you one."

As the last four words fell from his lips he looked for some change, slight and hardly perceptible perhaps, in the other's expression. But he was doomed to disappointment. The steady regard held, nothing moved about the man, not even the hand into which the poor disfigured chin had fallen. Ransom suppressed a sigh. His task was likely to prove a blind one. He had a sense of stumbling in the dark, but the gaze he had hoped to see falter compelled him to proceed, and he told his story without subterfuge or suppression.

One thing, and only one thing, caused a movement in the set figure before him. When he mentioned the will which Georgian had made a few hours prior to her disappearance, Hazen's hand slipped aside from the wound it had sought to cover, and Ransom caught sight of the sudden throb which deepened its hue. It was the one infallible sign that the man was not wholly without feeling, and it had sprung to life at an intimation involving money.

When his tale was quite finished, he rose. So did Hazen.

"Let us see this girl," suggested the latter.

It was the first word he had spoken since Ransom began his story.

"She is up-stairs. I will go see—"

"No, we will go see. I particularly desire to take her unawares."

Ransom offered no objection. Perhaps he felt interested in the experiment himself. Together they left the room, together they went up-stairs. A turmoil of questions followed them from the throng of men and boys gathered in the halls, but they returned no answer and curiosity remained unsatisfied.

Once in the hall above, Ransom stopped a moment to deliberate. He could not enter Anitra's room unannounced, and he could not make her hear by knocking. He must find the landlady.

He knew Mrs. Deo's room. He had had more than one occasion to visit it during the last two days. With a word of explanation to Hazen, he passed down the hall and tapped on the last door at the extreme left. No one answered, but the door standing ajar, he pushed it quietly open, being anxious to make sure that Mrs. Deo was not there.

The next moment he was beckoning to Hazen.

"Look!" said he, holding the door open with one hand and pointing with the other to a young girl sitting on a low stool by the window, mending, or trying to mend, a rent in her skirt.

"Why, that's Georgian!" exclaimed Hazen, and hastily entering he approached the anxious figure laboriously pushing her needle in and out of the torn goods, and pricking herself more than once in the attempt.

"Georgian!" he cried again and yet more emphatically, as he stepped up in front of her.

The young girl failed to notice. Awkwardly drawing her thread out to its extreme length, she prepared to insert her needle again, when her eye caught sight of his figure bending over her, and she looked up quietly and with an air of displeasure, which pleased Ransom,—he could hardly tell why. This was before her eyes reached his face; when they had, it was touching to see how she tried to hide the shock caused by its deformity, as she said with a slight gesture of dismissal:

"I'm quite deaf. I cannot hear what you say. If it is the landlady you want, she has gone down-stairs for a minute; perhaps, to the kitchen."

He did not retreat, if anything he approached nearer, and Ransom was surprised to observe the force and persuasive power of his expression as he repeated:

"No nonsense, Georgian," opening and shutting his hands as he spoke, in curious gesticulations which her eye mechanically followed but which seemed to convey no meaning to her, though he evidently expected them to and looked surprised (Ransom almost thought baffled) when she shook her head and in a sweet, impassive way reiterated:

"I cannot hear and I do not understand the deaf and dumb alphabet. I'm sorry, but you'll have to go to some one else. I'm very unfortunate. I have to mend this dress and I don't know how."

Hazen, who could hardly tear his eyes from her face, fell slowly back as she painfully and conscientiously returned to her task. "Good God!" he murmured, as his eye sought Ransom's. "What a likeness!" Then he looked again at the girl, at the wave of her raven black hair breaking into little curls just above her ear; at the smooth forehead rendered so distinguished by the fine penciling of her arching brows; at the delicate nose with nostrils all alive to the beating of an over-anxious heart; at the mouth, touching in its melancholy so far beyond her years; and lastly at the strong young figure huddled on the little stool; and bending forward again, he uttered two or three quick sentences which Ransom could not catch.

His persistence, or the near approach of his face to hers, angered her. Rising quickly to her feet, she vehemently cried out:

"Go away from here. It is not right to keep on talking to a deaf girl after she has told you she cannot hear you." Then catching sight of Ransom, who had advanced a step in his sympathy for her, she gave a little sigh of relief and added querulously:

"Make this man go away. This is the landlady's room. I don't like to have strangers talk to me. Besides—" here her voice fell, but not so low as to be inaudible to the subject of her remark, "he's not pretty. I've seen enough of men and women who are—"

At this point Ransom drew Hazen out into the hall.

"What do you think now?" he demanded.

Hazen did not reply. The room they had just left seemed to possess a strange fascination for him. He continued to look back at it as he preceded Ransom down the hall. Ransom did not press his questions, but when they were on the point of separating at the head of the stairs, he held Hazen back with the words:

"Let us come to some understanding. Neither of us can desire to waste strength in wrong conclusions. Can that woman be other than your own sister?"

"No." The denial was absolute. "She is my sister."

"Anitra?" emphasized Ransom.

The smile which he received in reply was strangely mirthless.

"I never rush to conclusions," was Hazen's remark after a moment of possibly mutual heart-beat and unsettling suspense. "Ask me that same question to-morrow. Perhaps by then I shall be able to answer you."

CHAPTER XX

BETWEEN THE ELDERBERRY BUSHES

"No."

The word came from Ransom. He had reached the end of his patience and was determined to have it out with this man on the spot.

"Come into my room," said he. "If you doubt her, you doubt me; and in the present stress of my affairs this demands an immediate explanation."

"I have no time to enter your room, and I cannot linger here any longer talking on a subject which at the present moment is not clear to either of us," was the resolute if not quite affable reply. "Later, when my conclusions are made, I will see you again. Now I am going to eat and refresh myself. Don't follow me; it will do you no good."

He turned to descend. Ransom had an impulse to seize him by his twisted throat and drag from him the secret which his impassive features refused to give up. But Ransom was no fool and, stepping back out of the way of temptation, he allowed him to escape without further parley.

Then he went to his room. But, after an hour or two spent with his own thoughts, his restlessness became so great that he sought the gossips below for relief. He found them all clustered about Hazen, who was reeling off stories by the mile. This was unendurable to him and he was striding off, when Hazen burst away from his listeners and, joining Ransom, whispered in his ear:

"I saw her go by the window just now on her way up-street. What can she find there to interest her? Where is she going?"

"I don't know. She doesn't consult me as to her movements. Probably she has gone for a walk. She looks as if she needs it."

"So do you," was the unexpected retort given by Hazen, as he stepped back to rejoin his associates.

Ransom paused, watching him askance in doubt of the suggestion, in doubt of the man, in doubt of himself. Then he yielded to an impulse stronger than any doubt and slipped out into the highway, where he turned, as she had turned, up-street.

But not without a struggle. He hated himself for his puppet-like acceptance of the hint given him by a man he both distrusted and disliked. He felt his dignity impaired and his self-confidence shaken, yet he went on, following the high road eagerly and watching with wary eye for the first glimpse of the slight figure which was beginning to make every scene alive to him.

It had rained heavily and persistently the last time he came this way, but to-day the sun was shining with a full radiance, and the trees stretching away on either side of the road were green with the tender tracery of early leafage; a joy-compelling sight which may have accounted for the elasticity of his step as he ascended one small hill after another in the wake of a fluttering skirt.

It was the cemetery road, and odd as the fancy was, he felt that he should overtake her at the old gate, behind which lay so many of her name. Here he had seen her name before its erasement from the family monument, and here he should see—could he say Anitra if he found her bending over those graves; the woman who could not hear, who could not read,—whose childish memory, if she had any in connection with this spot, could not be distinct enough or sufficiently intelligent to guide her to this one plot? No. Human credulity can go far, but not so far as that. He knew that all his old doubts would return if, on entering the cemetery, he found her under the brown shaft carved with the name of Hazen.

The test was one he had not sought and did not welcome. Yet he felt bound, now that he recognized it as such, to see it through and accept its teaching for what it surely would be worth. Only he began to move with more precaution and studied more to hide his approach than to give any warning of it.

The close ranks of the elderberry bushes lining the fences on the final hill-top lent themselves to the concealment he now sought. As soon as he was sure of her having left the road he drew up close to these bushes and walked under them till he was almost at the gate. Then he allowed himself to peer through their close branches and received an unexpected shock at seeing her figure standing very near him, posed in an uncertainty which, for some reason, he had not expected, but which restored him to himself, though why he had not the courage, the time, nor the inclination to ask.

She was babbling in a low tone to herself, an open sesame to her mind, which Ransom hailed with a sense of awe. If only he might distinguish the words! But this was difficult; not only was her head turned partly away, but she spoke in a murmur which was far from distinct. Yet—yes, that one sentence was plain enough. She had muttered musingly, anxiously, and with a searching look among the graves:

"It was on this side. I know it was on this side."

Watching her closely lest some chance glance of hers should stray his way, he listened still more intently and was presently rewarded by catching another sentence.

"A single grave all by itself. I fell over it and my mother scolded me, saying it was my father's. There was a bush near it. A bush with white flowers on it. I tried to pick some."

Ransom's heart was growing lighter and lighter. She did not even know that there had been placed over that grave a monument with her name on it and that of the mother who had scolded her for tripping over her father's sod. Only Anitra could be so ignorant or expect to find a grave by means of a bush blooming with flowers fifteen years ago. As she went wandering on, peering to right and left, he thought of Hazen and his doubts, and wished that he were here beside him to mark her perplexity.

When quite satisfied that she would never find what she sought without help, Ransom stepped from his hiding-place and joined her among the grassy hillocks. The start of pleasure she gave and her almost childish look of relief warmed his heart, and it was with a smile he waited for her to speak.

"My father's grave!" she explained. "I was looking for my father's grave. I remember my mother taking me to it when I was little. There was a bush close by it—oh! I see what you think. The bush would be big now—I forgot that. And something else! You are thinking of something else. Oh, I know, I know. He wouldn't be lying alone any more. My mother must have died, or sister would have taken me to her. There ought to be two graves."

He nodded, and taking her by the hand led her to the family monument. She gazed at it for a moment, amazed, then laid her finger on one of the inscriptions.

"My father's name?" she asked.

He nodded.

She hung her head thoughtfully for a moment, then slipping to the other side of the stone laid her hand on another.

"My mother's?"

Again he signified yes.

"And this? Is this sister's name? No, she's not buried yet. I had a brother. Is it his?"

Ransom bowed. How tell her that it was a false inscription and that the man whose death it commemorated was not only alive but had only a little while before spoken to her.

"I didn't like my brother. He was cruel and liked to hurt people. I'm glad he's dead."

Ransom drew her away. Her frankness was that of a child, but it produced an uncomfortable feeling. He didn't like this brother either, and in this thoughtless estimate of hers he seemed to read a warning to which his own nature intuitively responded.

"Come!" he motioned, leading the way out.

She followed with a smile, and together they entered the highway. As they did so, Ransom caught sight of a man speeding down the hill before them on a bicycle. He had not come front the upper road, or they would have seen him as he flew past the gateway. Where had he come from, then? From the peep-hole where Ransom himself had stood a few minutes before. No other conclusion was possible, and Ransom felt both angry and anxious till he could find out who the man was. This he did not succeed in doing till he reached the hotel. There a bicycle leaning against a tree gave point to his questions, and he learned that it belonged to a clerk in one of the small stores nearby, but that the man who had just ridden it up and down the road on a trial of speed was the stranger who had just come to town with Mr. Hazen.

CHAPTER XXI

ON THE CARS

This episode, which to Ransom's mind would bear but one interpretation, gave him ample food for thought. He decided to be more circumspect in the future and to keep an eye out for inquisitive strangers. Not that he had any thing to conceal, but no man enjoys having his proceedings watched, especially where a woman is concerned.

That Hazen was antagonistic to him he had always known; but that he was regarded by him with suspicion he had not realized till now. Hazen suspicious of him! that meant what? He wished that he had Mr. Harper at his side to enlighten him.

It was now five o'clock and he was sitting in his room awaiting the usual report from the river, when a quick tap at his door was followed by the entrance of the very man he was thinking about. He rose eagerly to receive him, determined, however, to allow no inconsiderate impulse to drive him into unnecessary speech.

"I have already said too much," he reminded himself in self-directed monition. "It's time he did some of the talking."

Hazen seemed willing enough to do this. Taking the seat proffered him, he opened the conversation as follows:

"Mr. Ransom, I have been doing you an injustice. I do not consider it necessary to tell you just how I have found this out, but I am now convinced that you are as much in the dark as myself in regard to this unfortunate affair, and are as willing as I am to take all justifiable means to enlighten yourself. I own that at first I thought it more than probable you were in collusion with the girl here to deceive me. That I wouldn't stand. I'm glad to find you as truly a victim of this mystery as myself."

Ransom straightened himself.

"If this is an apology," he returned, "I am willing to accept it in the spirit in which it is proffered. But I should like something more than apology from you. Candor for candor;—your whole story in return for mine."

"I'm afraid it would be a trifle tedious,—my whole story," smiled Hazen. "If you mean such part of it as concerns Georgian's peculiar actions and the complications with which we are at this moment struggling, I can only repeat what I have already told you, both at the St. Denis in New York and here. I am Georgian's returned brother, saved from the jaws of hell to see my own country again. I arrived in New York on the tenth. Naturally, after securing a room at the hotel, I took up the papers. They were full of the approaching marriage of Miss Hazen. I recognized my sister's name, though not her splendor, for we were the sole survivors of a poor country family and I knew nothing of the legacy I am now told she received. Anxious to see her, I attended the ceremony. She recognized me. I had not expected this, and feeling old affections revive, I followed her friends to the house and was presented to them and to you. What I whispered to her on this occasion were my assumed name and the place where I was to be found. My changed countenance called for explanations, for which a bridal reception offered no opportunity. Besides, as I have already said, I stood in sore need of a definite amount of money. I meant her to come and see me, but I did not expect her to play a trick on you in order to do so. This had its birth in the to me unaccountable mystery embodied in the girl you call Anitra, but whom I'm not ready yet to name. For when I do, action must follow conviction and that without mercy or delay."

"Action?" repeated Ransom, with quick suspicion and a confused rush of contradictory visions in his mind. "What do you mean by that?"

Hazen covered his chin with his hand.

"I will try and explain," he replied. "If I am abrupt in my language, it is owing to the exigencies of the case. I have no time to waste and no disposition to whitewash a rough piece of work. To speak to the point, I have an intense interest in my sister Georgian. I have little or none in my sister Anitra. Georgian's intelligence, good-will, and command of money would be of inestimable benefit to me. Anitra, on the contrary, could be nothing but a burden, unless—" here he cast a very sharp glance at Ransom—"unless Georgian should have been sufficiently considerate to leave her a good share of her fortune in the will you say she made just before her disappearance and supposed death."

"That I can say nothing about," rejoined Ransom in answer to this feeler. "The will is in the hands of her lawyer, but if it will help your argument any we will suppose that she left her sister to the care of her friends without any especial provision for her in the way of money."

The steady fingers clutching the scarred neck loosed their grip to wave this supposition aside.

"A hardly supposable case," was the cold comment with which he supplemented this disclaimer; "but one which would make the girl a burden indeed; a burden which for many reasons I could not assume." Here he struck himself sharply on the neck, with the first display of passion he had shown. "My advantages are not such as to make it easy for me to support myself. It would be simply impossible for me to undertake the care of any girl, least of all of one with a manifest infirmity."

"Anitra will prosper without your care," replied Ransom, overlooking the heartlessness of the man in the mad, unaccountable sense of relief with which he listened to his withdrawal from concerns for which he showed so little sympathy. "There are others who will be glad to do all that can be done for Georgian's forsaken sister."

"Yes. That is all right, but—" Here Hazen squared himself across the top of the table before which he had been sitting; "I must be made sure that the facts have been rightly represented to me and that the girl now in this house is Georgian's deserted sister. I'm not yet satisfied that she is, and I must be convinced not only on this point but on many others, before this day is over. Business of great importance calls me back to the city and, it may be, out of the country. I may never be able to spend another day on purely personal affairs, so this one must tell. I have a scheme (it is a very simple one) which, if carried out as I have planned, will satisfy me as nothing else will as to the identity of the girl we will call, from lack of positive knowledge, Anitra. Will you help me in its furtherance? It lies with you to do so."

"First, your reasons for doubting the girl," retorted Ransom. "They must be excellent ones for you to resist the evidence of such conclusive proofs as you have yourself been witness to since entering this house. I am Georgian's husband. I have the strongest wish in the world to see her again at my side; yet with the exception of her wonderful likeness to my wife, I find nothing in this raw if beautiful girl, of the polished, highly trained woman I married. I have not even succeeded in startling her ear—something which I should have been able to do if she were not the totally deaf woman she appears. Confide to me then your reasons for demanding additional proofs of her identity. If they carry conviction with them, I will aid you in any scheme you can propose which will neither frighten nor afflict her."

Hazen rose to his feet. Narrow as the room was, he yielded to his restless desire to move about and began pacing up and down the restricted quarters bounded by the edge of the table and the door. Not until he had made the second turning did he speak; then it was with seeming openness.

"It's like putting the torch to my last ship," said he; "but this is no time to hesitate. Mr. Ransom, I do not trust my eyes, I do not trust my ears, nor your eyes, nor your ears, nor those of any one here, because I have talked with a man who was on the same train with my sisters. He noticed them because of their similar appearance and close intimacy. They were not dressed alike, but they were veiled alike and one did not move without the other. More than that, they not only walked about the various stations where they waited, arm in arm, but they sat thus closely joined in the cars all the way from New York. This interested him especially as he noted great anxiety and incessant movement in the one, and complete passiveness in the other. She who sat in the outer seat was watchful, busy, and ready to press the other's arm at the least provocation, but if either spoke it was always the other. It was not till the quick rush and shrill whistle of a passing train made one start and not the other, that he got the idea that one of them was deaf. As this was the one by the window, he felt that their peculiar actions were now accounted for, and indeed thus far it all tallied with what we might expect from Georgian traveling with the hapless Anitra. But there remained a fact to be told, which rouses doubt. When they reached G— and he saw from their quick rising that they were about to leave the train, he naturally glanced their way again, and this time he caught a glimpse of the inner one's neck. Her veil had become slightly disarranged, exposing the whole nape. It was unexpectedly dark, almost brunette in color, and quite devoid of delicacy; such a skin as one might look for in the gipsy Anitra after years of outdoor living and a long lack of nice personal attention, but not such as I saw and admired a few hours ago on the neck of the woman bending over her work in the landlady's room. Oh, I recognized the difference; I have an eye for necks."

He paused, coming to a standstill in the middle of the room, to see what effect his words had had on Ransom.

"I have that man's name," he continued, "and can produce him if I have time and it seems to be necessary. But I had rather come to my own decision without any outside interference. This is not an affair for public gossip or newspaper notoriety. It is a question of justice to myself. If this girl is Georgian—" His whole face changed. For a moment Ransom hardly knew him. The quiet, self-contained man seemed to have given way to one of such unexpected power and threat that Ransom rose instinctively to his feet in recognition of a superiority he could no longer deny.

The action seemed to recall Hazen to himself. He wheeled about and recommenced his quiet pacing to and fro.

"I beg pardon," he quietly finished. "If it is Georgian, she must stand my friend. That is all I was going to say. If it is, against all reason and probability, her strangely restored twin, I shall leave this house by midnight, never probably to see any of you again. So you perceive that it is incumbent upon us to work promptly. Are you ready to hear what I have to propose?"

"Yes."

Hazen paused again, this time in front of the door. Laying his hand lightly on one of the panels, he glanced back at Ransom.

"You are nicely placed here for observation. Your door directly faces the hall she must traverse in returning to her room."

"That's quite true."

"She's in her room now. Ah, you know that?"

"Yes." Ransom seemed to have no other word at his command.

"Will she come out again before night to eat or to visit?"

"There's no telling. She's very fitful. No one can prophesy what she will do. Sometimes she eats in the landlady's room, sometimes in her own, sometimes not at all. If you have frightened her, or she has been disturbed in any way by your companion who shows such interest in her and in me, she probably will not come out at all."

"But she must. I expect you to see that she does. Use any messenger, any artifice, but get her away from this hall for ten minutes, even if it is only into Mrs. Deo's room. When she returns I shall be on my knees before this keyhole to watch her and observe. To see what, I do not mean to tell you, but it will be something which will definitely settle for me this matter of identity. Does this plan look sufficiently harmless to meet with your approval?"

"Yes, but looks cannot always be trusted. I must know just what you mean to do. I will leave nothing to a mind and hand I do not trust any more fully than I do yours. You are too eager for Georgian's money; too little interested in herself; and you are too sly in your ways. I overlooked this when you had the excuse of a possible distrust of myself. But now that your confidence is restored in me, now that you recognize the fact that I stand outside of this whole puzzling affair and have no other wish than to know the truth about it and do my duty to all parties concerned, secrecy on your part means more than I care to state. If you persist in it I shall lend myself to nothing that you propose, but wait for time to substantiate her claim or prove its entire falsity."

"You will!"

The words rang out involuntarily. It almost seemed as if the man would spring with them straight at the other's throat. But he controlled himself, and smiling bitterly, added:

"I know the marks of human struggle. I have read countenances from my birth. I've had to, and only one has baffled me—hers. But we are going to read that too and very soon. We are going to learn, you and I, what lies behind that innocent manner and her rude, uncultivated ways. We are going to sound that deafness. I say we," he impressively concluded, "because I have reconsidered my first impulse and now propose to allow you to participate openly, and without the secrecy you object to, in all that remains to be done to make our contemplated test a success. Will that please you? May I count on you now?"

"Yes," replied Ransom, returning to his old monosyllable.

"Very well, then, see if you can make a scrawl like this."

Pulling a piece of red chalk from his pocket, he drew a figure of a somewhat unusual character on the bare top of the table between them; then he handed the chalk over to Ransom, who received it with a stare of wonder not unmixed with suspicion.

"I'm not an adept at drawing," said he, but made his attempt, notwithstanding, and evidently to Hazen's satisfaction.

"You'll do," said he. "That's a mystic symbol once used by Georgian and myself in place of our names in all mutual correspondence, and on the leaves of our school-books and at the end of our exercises. It meant nothing, but the boys and girls we associated with thought it did and envied us the free-masonry it was supposed to cover. A ridiculous make-believe which I rate at its full folly now, but one which cannot fail to arouse a hundred memories in Georgian. We will scrawl it on her door, or rather you shall, and according to the way she conducts herself on seeing it, we shall know in one instant what you with your patience and trust in time may not be able to arrive at in weeks."

Ransom recalled some of the tests he had himself employed, many of which have been omitted from this history, and shrugged his shoulders mentally, if not physically. If Hazen noted this evidence of his lack of faith, he remained entirely unaffected by it, and in a few minutes everything had been planned between them for the satisfactory exercise of what Hazen evidently regarded as a crucial experiment. Ransom was about to proceed to take the first required step, when they heard a disturbance in front, and the coach came driving up with a great clatter and bang and from it stepped the lean, well-groomed figure of Mr. Harper.

"Bah!" exclaimed Hazen with a violent gesture of disappointment. "There comes your familiar. Now I suppose you will cry off."

"Not necessarily," returned Ransom. "But this much is certain. I shall certainly consult him before hazarding this experiment. I am not so sure of myself or—pardon me—of yourself as to take any steps in the dark while I have at hand so responsible a guide as the man whom you choose to call my familiar."

CHAPTER XXII

A SUSPICIOUS TEST

"Let him make his experiment. It will do no harm, and if it rids us of him, well and good."

Such was Mr. Harper's decision after hearing all that Mr. Ransom had to tell him of the present situation.

"His disappointment when he learns that he has nothing to hope for from his sister's generosity calls for some consideration from us," proceeded the lawyer. "Go and have your little talk with the landlady or take whatever other means suggest themselves for luring this girl from her room. I will summon Hazen and hold him very closely under my eye till the whole affair is over. He shall get no chance for any hocus-pocus business, not while I have charge of your interests. He shall do just what he has laid out for himself and nothing more; you may rely on that."

Ransom expressed his satisfaction, and left the room with a lighter heart than he had felt since Hazen came upon the scene. He did not know that all he had been through was as nothing to what lay before him.

It was an hour before he returned. When he did, it was to find Hazen and the lawyer awaiting him in ill-concealed impatience. These two were much too incongruous in tastes and interests to be very happy in a forced and prolonged tête-à-tête.

"Have you done it?" exclaimed Hazen, leaping eagerly to his feet as the door closed softly behind Ransom. "Is she out of her room? I have listened and listened for her step, but could not be sure of it. There seem to be a lot of people in the house to-night."

"Too many," quoth Ransom. "That is why I couldn't get hold of Mrs. Deo any sooner. Anitra is having her hair brushed or something else of equal importance done for her in one of the rear rooms. So we can proceed fearlessly. Have you looked to see if you can get a good glimpse of her door through the keyhole of this one?"

"Haven't you already made a trial of that? Then do so now," suggested Hazen, drawing out the key and laying it on the table.

But this was too uncongenial a task for Ransom.

"I shall be satisfied," said he, "if Mr. Harper tells me that it can."

"It can," asserted that gentleman, falling on his knees and adjusting his eye to the keyhole. "Or rather, you can see plainly the face of any one approaching it. I don't suppose any of us expected to see the door itself."

"No, it is not the door, but the woman entering the door, we want to see. Did you ask for an extra lamp?"

"Yes, and saw it placed. It is on a small table almost opposite her room."

"Then everything is ready."

"All but the mark which I am to put on the panel."

"Very good. Here is the chalk. Let us see what you mean to do with it before you risk an attempt on the door itself."

Ransom thought a minute, then with one quick twist produced the following:

"Correct," muttered Hazen, with what Harper thought to be a slight but unmistakable shudder. "One would think you had been making use of this very cabalistic sign all your life."

"Then one would be mistaken. I have simply a true eye and a ready hand."

"And a very remarkable memory. You have recalled every little line and quirk."

"That's possible. What I have made once I can make the second time. It's a peculiarity of mine."

There was no mistaking the continued intensity of Hazen's gaze. Ransom felt his color rise, but succeeded in preserving his quiet tone, as he added:

"Besides, this character is not a wholly new one to me. My attention was called to it months ago. It was when I was courting Georgian. She was writing a note one day when she suddenly stopped to think and I saw her pen making some marks which I considered curious. But I should not have remembered them five minutes, if she had not impulsively laid her hand over them when she saw me looking. That fixed the memory of them in my mind, and when I saw this combination of lines again, I remembered it. That is why I lent myself so readily to this experiment. I lent that what you said about her acquaintance with this odd arrangement of lines was true."

Hazen's hand stole up to his neck, a token of agitation which Ransom should have recognized by this time.

"And her account of the use we made of it tallied with mine?"

"She gave me no account of any use she had ever made of it."

"That was because you didn't ask her."

"Just so. Why should I ask her? It was a small matter to trouble her about."

"You are right," acquiesced Hazen, wheeling himself away towards the window. Then after a momentary silence, "It was so then, but it is likely to prove of some importance now. Let me see if the hall is empty."

As he bent to open the door, the lawyer, who had not moved nor spoken till now, turned a quick glance on Ransom and impulsively stretched out his hand. But he dropped it very quickly and subsided into his old attitude of simple watchfulness, as Hazen glanced back with the remark:

"There's nobody stirring; now's your time, Ransom."

The moment for action had arrived.

Ransom stepped into the hall. As he passed Hazen, the latter whispered:

"Don't forget that last downward quirk. That was the line she always emphasized."

Ransom gave him an annoyed look. His nerves as well as his feelings were on a keen stretch, and this persistence of Hazen's was more than he could bear.

"I'll not forget the least detail," he answered shortly, and passed quickly down the hall, while Hazen watched him through the crack of the door, and the lawyer watched Hazen.

Suddenly Mr. Harper's brow wrinkled. Hazen had uttered such a sigh of relief that the lawyer was startled. In another moment Ransom re-entered the room.

"She's coming," said he, striving to hide his extreme emotion. "I heard her voice in the hall beyond."

Hazen sprang to the door which Ransom had carefully closed, and was about to fall on his knees before the keyhole when he suddenly stiffened himself and, turning towards the lawyer, cried with a new strain of loftiness in his tone:

"You. You shall do the looking, only promise to be very minute in your description of her behavior. It's a great trust I repose in you. See that you honor it."

The revulsion of feeling caused in the lawyer by this show of confidence was not perceptible. But it softened his step as well as his manner as he crossed to do the other's bidding.

The remaining two stood at his side breathless, waiting for his first word.

It came in a whisper:

"She's approaching her room. She looks tired. Her eyes are stealing this way;—no, they are resting on her own door. She sees the sign. She stands staring at it, but not like a person who has ever seen it before. It's the stare of an uneducated woman who runs upon something she does not understand. Now she touches it with one finger and glances up and down the hall with a doubtful shake of the head. Now she is running to another door, now to another. She is looking to see if this scrawl is to be found anywhere else; she even casts her eye this way—I feel like leaving my post. If I do, you may know that she's coming—No, she's back at her own door and—gentlemen, her bringing up or rather coming up asserts itself. She has put her palm to her mouth and is vigorously rubbing off the marks."

The next instant Mr. Harper rose. "She's gone into her room," said he. "Listen and you will hear her key click in the lock."

Ransom sank into a seat; Hazen had walked to the window. Presently he turned.

"I am convinced," said he. "I will not trouble you gentlemen further. Mr. Ransom, I condole with you upon your loss. My sister was a woman of uncommon gifts."

Mr. Ransom bowed. He had no words for this man at a moment of such extreme excitement. He did not even note the latent sting hidden in the other's seeming tribute to Georgian. But the lawyer did and Hazen perceived that he did, for pausing in his act of crossing the room, he leaned for a moment on the table with his eyes down, then quickly raising them remarked to that gentleman:

"I am going to leave by the midnight train for New York. To-morrow I shall be on the ocean. Will it be transgressing all rules of propriety for me to ask the purport of my sister's will? It is a serious matter to me, sir. If she has left me anything—"

"She has not," emphasized the lawyer.

A shadow darkened the disappointed man's brow. His wound swelled and his eyes gleamed ironically as he turned them upon Ransom.

Instantly that gentleman spoke.

"I have received but a moiety," said he. "You need not envy me the amount."

"Who has it then?" briskly demanded the startled man. "Who? who? She?"

Mr. Harper never knew why he did it. He was reserved as a man and, usually, more than reserved as a lawyer, but as Hazen lifted his hands from the table and turned to leave, he quietly remarked:

"The chief legatee—the one she chose to leave the bulk of her very large fortune to—is a man we none of us know. His name is Josiah Auchincloss."

The change which the utterance of this name caused in Hazen's expression threw them both into confusion.

"Why didn't you tell me that in the beginning?" he cried. "I needn't have wasted all this time and effort."

His eyes shone, his poor lips smiled, his whole air was jubilant. Both Mr. Harper and his client surveyed him in amazement. The lines so fast disappearing from his brow were beginning to reappear on theirs.

"Mr. Harper," this hard-to-be-understood man now declared, "you may safely administer the estate of my sister. She is surely dead."

CHAPTER XXIII

A STARTLING DECISION

Before Mr. Ransom and the lawyer had recovered from their astonishment, Hazen had slipped from the room. As Mr. Harper started to follow, he saw the other's head disappearing down the staircase leading to the office. He called to him, but Hazen declined to turn.

"No time," he shouted back. "I shall have to make use of somebody's automobile now, to get to the Ferry in time."

The lawyer did not persist, not at that moment; he went back to his client and they had a few hurried words; then Mr. Harper went below and took up his stand on the portico. He was determined that Hazen should not leave the place without some further explanation.

It was light where he stood and he very soon felt that this would not do, so he slipped back into the shade of a pillar, and seeing, from the bustle, that Hazen was likely to obtain the use of the one automobile stored in the stable, he waited with reasonable patience for his reappearance in the road before him.

Meanwhile he had confidence in Ransom, who he felt sure was watching them both from the window overhead. If he should fail in getting in the word he wanted, Ransom was pledged to shout it out without regard to appearances. But this was not likely to occur. He knew his own persistency to equal Hazen's. Nothing should stop the momentary interview he had promised himself.

Ah! A well-known whirr and clatter is heard. The automobile was leaving the stable. Hazen was already in it and the man who had come up from New York was with him. This was bad; they would flash by— No; he would not be balked thus. Stepping out into the road, he stopped full in the glare of the office lights and held up his hand. They could not but see him and they did. The chauffeur reversed the lever and the machine stopped to the accompaniment of low muttered oaths from Hazen, which were rather disagreeable than otherwise to Harper's ear.

"One word," said he, approaching to the side where Hazen sat. "I thought you ought to know before leaving that we can take no proceedings in the matter we were speaking of till we have undisputed proof that your sister is dead. That we may not get for a long time, possibly never. If you are interested in having this Auchincloss receive his inheritance, you had better prepare both yourself and him for a long wait. The river seems slow to give up its dead."

The quiver of impatience which had shaken Hazen at the first word had settled into a strange rigidity.

"One moment," he said in a command to the chauffeur at his side. Then in a low, strangely sounding whisper to Harper: "They think the body's in the Devil's Cauldron. Nothing can get it out if it is. Would some proof of its presence there be sufficient to settle the fact of her death?"

"That would depend. If the proof was unmistakable, it might pass in the Surrogate's Court. What is the matter, Hazen?"

"Nothing." The tone was hollow; the whole man sat like an image of death. "I—I'm thinking—weighing—" he uttered in scattered murmurs. Then suddenly, "You're not deceiving me, Harper. Some proof will be necessary, and that very soon, for this man Auchincloss to realize the money?"

"Yes," the monosyllable was as dry as it was short. Harper's patience with this unnatural brother was about at an end.

"And who will venture to obtain this proof for us? No one. Not even Ransom would venture down into that watery hole. They say it is almost certain death," babbled Hazen.

Harper kept silence. Strange forces were at work. The head of another gruesome tragedy loomed vaguely through the shadows of this already sufficiently tragic mystery.

"Go on!" suddenly shouted Hazen, leaning forward to the chauffeur. But the next instant his hand was on the man's sleeve. "No, I have changed my mind. Here, Staples," he called out as a man came running down the steps, "take my bag and ask the landlady to prepare me a room. I'll not try for the train to-night." Then as the man at his side leaped to the ground, he turned to Harper and remarked quietly, but in no common tone:

"The steamer must sail without me. I'll stay in this place a while and prove the death of Georgian Ransom myself."

CHAPTER XXIV

THE DEVIL'S CAULDRON

The solemnity of Hazen's whole manner impressed Mr. Harper strongly. As soon as the opportunity offered he cornered the young man in the office where he had taken refuge, and giving him to understand that further explanations must pass between them before either slept, he drew him apart and put the straight question to him:

"Who is Josiah Auchincloss?"

The answer was abrupt, almost menacing in its emphasis and tone.

"A trunk-maker in St. Louis. A man she was indebted to."

"How indebted to—a trunk-maker?"

"That I cannot, do not desire to state. It is enough that she felt she owed him the bulk of her fortune. Though this eliminates me from benefits of a wealth I had some rights to share, I make no complaint. She knew her business best, and I am disposed to accept her judgment in the matter without criticism."

"You are?" The tone was sharp, the sarcasm biting. "I can understand that. For Auchincloss, in this will, read Hazen; but how about her husband? How about her friends and the general community? Do you not think they will ask why a beautiful and socially well-placed young woman like your sister should leave so large a portion of her wealth to an obscure man in another town, of whom her friends and even her business agent have never heard? It would have been better if she had left you her thousands directly."

The smile which was Hazen's only retort was very bitter.

"You drew up her will," said he. "You must have reasoned with her on this very point as you are now trying to reason with me?"

The lawyer waved this aside.

"I didn't know at that time the social status of the legatee; nor did I know her brother then as well as I do now."

"You do not know me now."

"I know that you are very pale; that the determination you have just made has cost you more than you perhaps are willing to state. That there is mystery in your past, mystery in your present, and, possibly, mystery threatening your future, and all in connection with your great desire for this money."

Hazen made a forcible gesture, but whether of denial or depreciation, it was not easy to decide.

"Would it not then be better for all parties," pursued the lawyer, "for you to give me some idea of the great obligation under which your sister lay to this man, that I may have an answer ready when people ask me why she passed you so conspicuously by, in order to enrich this stranger?"

"The story is not mine. Had she wished you to know it, she would have confided it to you herself. I must decline—"

Mr. Harper interrupted the other impressively. "Do you realize what a shadow may be thrown upon your sister's memory by this reticence on your part? Her death was suggestive enough without the complications you mention. In justice to your relationship you should speak. If, as I think, the money is really meant for you, say so. The subterfuge may be difficult of explanation, but it will not hurt her memory as much as this extraordinary silence on your part."

"I am sorry," began Hazen. But Harper cut him short.

"You expect the money—you yourself," said he. "Nothing else would force you into an attempt so perilous. You would risk death. Risk something less final; risk your place in my esteem, your standing among men, and confess the full truth about this matter. If it involves crime—why, I'm a lawyer and can see you through better than you can win through by your own misdirected efforts. The truth, my lad, the truth, nothing else will serve you."

The look he received he will never forget.

"You are a man of limited experience, Mr. Harper," were the words which accompanied it. "You would not understand the truth, Georgian or me. Ransom might, but I shall not even risk Ransom's discretion. Now this is all I am going to say about this matter. Georgian's last will and testament, followed though it was by suicide, was a perfectly regular one. The only impediment to its being so recognized and acted upon is the doubt as to her actual decease. If the body of my poor young sister has become lodged in the Devil's Cauldron, I am going there to seek it. As the project calls for courage and, above all, a good condition of body and mind, I shall be obliged to you if you will allow me the benefit of the sleep I most certainly need. To-morrow I may have something more to say to you, and I may not. Perhaps I shall want to make my will, who knows?" And with a smile full of sarcastic meaning, he pushed Mr. Harper's arm aside and made for the staircase, up which he presently vanished without another attempt on the lawyer's part to hold him back.

A few minutes later the lawyer was getting what information he could about the so-called Devil's Cauldron.

It seems that this was a very deep hole in which, on account of the rocky formation surrounding it, the water swept in an eddy which had the force of a whirlpool. No one had ever sounded its depths and nothing had ever been seen again which had once been sucked into its deathly hollow. That Georgian's body had found its everlasting grave there, many had believed from the first, and if the conviction had not yet been publicly expressed it was out of consideration for Mr. Ransom, to whose hopes it could but ring a final knell.

"Where is the hole? How far from the waterfall?" queried Mr. Harper.

"A good mile," muttered one man. "Quite around the bend of the stream. It's a horrid place, sir. We've always been mortal careful about rowing down that side of the river. Children are never allowed to. Only a man's strength could get him free again if he once struck the eddy."

"Would anything floating down from the falls be apt to strike this eddy?"

"Very apt. It would be a miracle if it didn't. That is why we all turned out so willingly the first day. We knew that if Mrs. Ransom's body was to be found at all, it would be found then; another day it would be beyond our reach."

"You say that no one has ever sounded the depths of that hole. Has any one ever tried to?"

"More than once. Scientific men and others."

"Did they ever emerge—any of them?"

"Yes, one, a powerful sort of chap with Indian blood in him. But he didn't advise any one to try it; said the knowledge wasn't worth the strain to heart and muscle."

"What was the knowledge? We can imagine the strain."

"Oh, he said as how the walls of the vortex—didn't he call it a vortex—was all stone, and he spoke of a ledge—I didn't hear what else."

"To go down there a man would have to take his life in his hand, I see. Well, I don't think I will try," dryly observed the lawyer as he left the room.

He could no longer hide his excitement at the thought that Hazen meditated this undertaking.

"How he must want money!" thought he. That a man should face such a horror for another man's profit did not seem likely enough to engage his consideration for a moment.

Lawyer Harper knew the world—or thought he did.

Next day the whole town was thrown into a hubbub. Word had gone out through every medium possible to so small a place, that Alfred Hazen, Georgian's long-lost brother, was going to dare Death Eddy in a final attempt to recover his sister's body.

PART IV

THE MAN OF MYSTERY

CHAPTER XXV

DEATH EDDY

It was a gray day, chill and ominous. As the three most interested in the event came together on the road facing the point from which Hazen had decided to make his desperate plunge, the dreariness of the scene was reflected in the troubled eye of the lawyer and that of the still more profoundly affected Ransom. Only Hazen gazed unmoved. Perhaps because the spot was no new one to him, perhaps because an unsympathetic sky, a stretch of rock, the swirl of churning waters without any of the lightness and color which glancing sunlight gives, meant for him but one thing—the thing upon which he had fixed his mind, his soul.

The rocky formation into which the stream ran at this point as into a pocket, revealed itself in the bald outlines of the point which, curving half-way upon itself, held in its cold embrace the unseen vortex. One tree, and one only, disturbed the sky line. Stark and twisted into an unusual shape from the steady blowing of the prevalent east winds, it imprinted itself at once upon the eye and unconsciously upon the imagination. To some it was the keeper of that hell-gate; the contorted sentinel of bygone woes and long-buried horrors, if not the gnomish genius of others yet to come. To-day it was the sign-post to a strange deed—the courting of an uncanny death that one of the many secrets hidden in that hole of miseries might be unlocked.

Under this tree a small group of strong and determined men was already collected; not as spectators but helpers in the adventurous attempt about to be undertaken by their old friend and playmate. The spectators had been barred from the point and stood lined up in the road overlooking the eddy. They were numerous and very eager. Hazen's brows drew together in his first exhibition of feeling, as he saw women and even children in the crowd, and caught the expression of morbid anticipation with which they all turned as he stepped with his two associates over the rope which had been stretched across the base of the out-curving head line.

"Cormorants!" escaped his lips. "They look for a feast of death, but they will be disappointed." He was almost bitter. "I shall survive this plunge. I have no wish for my death to be the holiday for a hundred gloating eyes, I am not handsome enough. When I die, it will be quietly, with some hand near, kind enough to cover my poor face with a napkin."

Harper and Ransom both remembered this remark a little while later.

"Mr. Hazen?" It was Harper who spoke. They had passed a little thicket of brush and were drawing near the group under the tree. "Have you duly considered what you are about to do? I have talked with several men of judgment and experience about this attempt, and they all say it can have but one termination."

"I know. That is because they know little or nothing of the life I have led since I left this town. There is not a man amongst them so slight and seemingly frail of figure as myself, but none of them, not one, has been so often up to the very gates of death and escaped, as I have. My schooling has been long and severe, perhaps in preparation for this day. I have been through fire; I have been through water. The swirling of my own native stream does not appall me. I rather welcome it; it is but another experience."

"But for money?" broke in Ransom. "You acknowledge it is for no other purpose. Will it pay? I own that in my eyes no amount of money could pay a man for so superhuman a risk as this. Take a few thousands from me—I had rather give them to you than see you leap into that water opening beneath us like a hungry maw."

Hazen stood silent, his eye glistening, his hand almost outstretched. Harper thought he would yield; the offer must have struck him as generous and very tempting—a good excuse for a hot-headed man to withdraw from a very doubtful adventure. But he did not know Hazen. This latter advanced his hand and squeezed Ransom's warmly, but his answer, when he was ready to give one, conveyed no intention of a change of mind.

"Will your thousands amount to a clean million?" he smiled. "That is the amount, I believe, bequeathed by your wife to Mr. Auchincloss. Nothing less will suffice. Yet I thank you, Ransom."

The latter bowed and fell a little behind the others. The struggle in his mind had been severe; it was severe yet; he did not know but that it was his duty to stop this Hazen from his intended action by force. He was not sure but that the onus of this whole desperate undertaking would yet fall upon him. Certainly it would fall upon his conscience if the end was fatal. He had had proof of that in the long night of wakeful misery he had just passed; a night in which he had faced the furies; in which this inexorable question had forced itself upon him despite every effort on his part to evade it.

Why had he, a humane man, consented to this attempt on the part of the devoted Hazen? That his mind might be free to mourn his beautiful young bride whose fatal and mysterious secret he was still as far from knowing as in the hour he turned to welcome her to their first home and found her fled from his arms and heart? Or had this suspense, this feeling of standing now, as never before, at the opening door of fate, a deeper significance, a more active meaning? Was this meditated test a crucial one, because it opened to him the only possible releasement of soul and conscience to the undivided care of one who had no other refuge in life save that offered by his devotion? The horror of this self-probing was still upon him as he followed Hazen's slight and virile figure across the rocks, but it fled as he felt the spray of the tossing waters dash its chilling reminder in his face.

The event was upon him and he must add to his former actions that of a complete and determined opposition to the risk proposed or possibly forfeit his peace of mind forever. Quickening his pace, he reached Hazen and the lawyer just as the men awaiting them had advanced on their side. Instantly he knew it was too late. There was neither time nor opportunity for any weak protests on his part now. Older men were speaking; men who knew the river, the danger, and the man, but even they said nothing to him in way of dissuasion. They only pointed out what especial points of suction were to be avoided, and showed him the chain they had brought for his waist and how he was to pull upon it the very instant he felt his senses or his strength leaving him.

He answered as a courageous man might, and making ready by taking off his coat and shoes he gave himself into their hands for the proper fastening on of the chain. Then, while the murmur of expectation rose from the crowd on the river bank, he stepped back to Mr. Ransom and whispered hurriedly in his ear:

"You have a good heart, a better heart than I ever gave you credit for. Promise that in case I never come out of those waters alive, that you will put no obstacle in the way of Mr. Auchincloss inheriting his fortune in good time. He's a man worthy of all the assistance which money can bring. You do not need her wealth; Anitra—well, she will be cared for, but Auchincloss—promise—brother."

Ransom half drew back in his amazement. Then started forward again. This man whom he had always distrusted, whom he had looked upon as Georgian's possible enemy, certainly his own, was looking into his eyes with a gaze of trust, almost of affection. The money was not for himself; he showed it by the noble, almost grand look with which he waited for his answer; a look that carried conviction despite Ransom's prejudice and great dislike.

"You will give me that much additional nerve for the task lying before me?" he added. And Ransom could only bow his head. The man's mastery was limitless; it had reached and moved even him.

Another moment and a gasp went up from fifty or more throats. Hazen had taken the chain in his hand, walked to the edge of the rock and slipped into the quietest water he saw there.

"Strike left!" called out a voice. And he struck left. The eddy seized him and they could see his head moving slowly about in the great circle which gradually grew smaller and smaller till he suddenly disappeared. A groan muffled with horror went up from the shore. But the man who held the chain lifted up his hand, and silence—more pregnant of anticipation than any sound—held that whole crowd rigid. The man played out the chain; Harper stared at the seething, tumbling water, but Ransom looked another way. The torture in his soul was taking shape, the shape of a ghost rising from those tossing waters. Suddenly the pent-in breath of fifty breasts found its way again to the lips.

The men who held the chain were pulling it in with violent reaches. It dragged more slowly, stuck, loosened itself, and finally brought into sight a face white as the foam it rose amongst.

"Dead! Drowned!" the whisper went around.

But when Hazen was dragged ashore and Ransom had thrown himself at his feet, he saw that he yet lived, and lived triumphantly. Ransom could not have told more; it was for others to see and point out the smile that sweetened the wan lips, and the passion with which he held against his breast some sodden and shapeless object which he had rescued from those awful depths, and which, when spread out and clean of sand, betrayed itself as that peculiar article of woman's clothing, a small side bag.

"I remember that bag," said Harper. "I saw it, or one exactly like it, in Mrs. Ransom's hand when she got into the coach the day we all rode up from the ferry. What will he have to say about it? and could he have seen the body from which it has evidently been torn?"

CHAPTER XXVI

HAZEN

"An unfathomable man," grumbled Mr. Harper, entering Mr. Ransom's room in marked disorder. "They say that he has not spoken yet; but the coroner is with him and we shall hear something from him soon. I expect—" here the lawyer's voice changed and his manner took on meaning—"that his report will be final."

"Final? You mean—"

"What his fainting face showed. For all its pallor and the exhaustion it expressed, there was triumph in its every feature. The little bag was not all he saw in that pit of hell. You must prepare yourself for no common ordeal, Ransom; it will take all your courage to listen to his story."

"I know." The words came with difficulty but not without a certain manly courage. "I shall try not to make you too much trouble." Then after a moment of oppressive silence, "Did you notice, when we all came in, the figure of a woman disappearing up the stair way? It was Anitra's and it paused before it reached the top, and I saw her eyes staring down at Hazen's helpless figure with a wildness in its inquiry that has sapped all my courage. How are we to answer that girl when she asks us what has happened? How make her know that Hazen is her brother and that he has just risked his life to satisfy himself and us that Georgian was really lost in that dreadful pool."

The lawyer, darting a keen glance at the speaker, softly shook his head.

"I am not thinking of Miss Hazen," said he. "I'm wondering how far the proof he has obtained will go." He paused, listening, then made a gesture towards the hall. "There's some one there," he whispered.

Ransom rose, and with a quick turn of the wrist pulled open the door.

A man was standing on the threshold, a ghastly figure before which Ransom involuntarily stepped back.

"Hazen!" he cried; then, as the other tottered, he sprang forward again and, reaching out his hand to steady him, drew him in with the remark, "We were expecting a summons from you. We are happy that you find yourself able to come to us."

"The coroner has just gone. The doctors I dismissed. I have something to say to you—to both of you," he added as he caught sight of Mr. Harper.

Entering slowly, he sat down in the chair proffered him by the lawyer. There was something strange in his air, a quiet automaton-like quality which attracted the latter's notice and led him to watch him very closely. Ransom was busy with the door, which the strong west wind blowing through the hall made difficult to close.

"I—" The one word uttered, Hazen seemed to forget himself. Sitting quite still, he gazed straight before him at the open window. There was little to be seen there but the swaying boughs of the huge tree, but his gaze never left those tossing limbs, and his sentence hung suspended till the movement made by Ransom recrossing the room roused him, and he went on.

"I have made the plunge, gentlemen, and fortune favored me. I—" here his voice failed him again, but realizing the fact more quickly than before, he shook off his apathy, and facing the two men, who awaited his slow words with inconceivable excitement, continued with sudden concentration upon his subject, "I saw what I went to see—poor Georgian's body. I have satisfied the coroner of this fact. The little bag I tore from her side proves her identity beyond a doubt. You saw it, Mr. Harper. They tell me that you recognized it at once as the same you saw in her hand in the stage-coach. But if you had not, the initials on it are unmistakable, G. Q. H., Georgian Quinlan Hazen. Auchincloss will get his money, and soon, will he not? Answer me plainly, Harper. Such an experience merits some reward. You will not make difficulties?"

"I?" The lawyer's query had a strange ring to it. He glanced from Hazen to Ransom, and from Ransom back to Hazen, whose features had now become more composed, though they still retained their remarkable pallor.

"If the proof is positive," he then went on, "you assuredly can trust both my client and myself to remember our promise to you."

"The coroner, you say, is satisfied?"

"Yes, with the proof and my sworn statement. He is obliged to be. No one else, least of all himself, feels any desire to go down to that whirling eddy for confirmation of my story. And they are wise. I do not think that any man with less experience than myself could sound the depths of that vortex and come up alive. The noise—the swirl—the sense of being sucked down—down in ever-increasing fury—but my purpose kept the life in me. I was determined not to yield, not to faint, till I had seen—and proved—"

"What's that?"

The cry was from Mr. Ransom. A sudden gust of wind had torn its way through the room, flinging the door wide, and strewing the floor with flying papers from the large stand in the window.

"Nothing but wind," answered Harper, half rising to close the door, but immediately sitting down again with a strange look at Ransom. "Let be," he whispered, as the other rose in his turn to restore order. "Keep Hazen talking. It's important; imperative. I'll see to the door."

But it was the window he closed, not the door.

Ransom, with that obedience natural to a client in presence of his most trusted adviser, did as he was bid, and turned his full attention back to Hazen instantly. That gentleman, upon whom the rushing wind and the havoc it created had made little if any impression, rushed again into words.

"I've led an adventurous life," he declared, "and, in the last few years especially, passed through many perils and experienced much awful suffering. I have felt the pang of hunger and the pang of biting despair; but nothing I have ever endured can equal the horror which beclouded my mind and rendered powerless my body as I felt myself sliding from the sight of earth and heaven into the jaws of that rapacious eddy, whose bottom no man had ever sounded.

"I went in young—I have come out old. Look at my hands—they shake like those of a man of ninety. Yet yesterday they could have pulled to the ground an ox."

"You saw Mrs. Ransom's body down in that pool some fathoms below the surface," observed the lawyer, after waiting in vain for some word from the shrinking husband. "Won't you particularize, Mr. Hazen? Tell us just how she was lying and where. Mr. Ransom cannot but wish to know, difficult as he evidently finds it to ask you."

"The coroner has the story," Hazen began, with the slow, painful gasp of the unwilling narrator. "But I will tell it again; it is your right, the painful duty which we cannot escape. She was lying, not on the bottom, but in a niche of rock into which she had been thrown and wedged by the force of the current. One arm was free and was washing about; I tried to clutch this arm as I went down, but it eluded me. When I arose, the rush and swirl of the water was against me and I felt my senses going, but enough instinct was left for me to snatch again at the arm as I passed, and though it eluded me again, my fingers closed on something, which I was just conscious enough to hold on to with a frenzied grip. We have spoken of this thing—a little bag which must have been fastened to her side, for the end of its connecting strap is torn away by the wrench I gave it."

"Vivid enough; but I am sure you will tell me one thing more. Did you see the face of this body as well as the arm? It would greatly add to the strength of your testimony if you could describe it."

Ransom, who had been watching Hazen, cast a sudden look back at the lawyer as he dropped these insinuating words. Something more than a cold-blooded desire for truth had prompted this almost brutal inquisition. He must know what it was, if anything in Harper's well-controlled countenance would tell him. The result transfixed him, for following the lawyer's gaze, which was fixed not on the man he was addressing but on a small mirror hanging on the opposite wall, he saw reflected in it the face and form of Anitra standing in the open doorway behind them.

She was looking at Hazen and, as Ransom noted that look, he understood Harper's previous caution and all that lay behind his insistent and cold-blooded questions. For her gaze was no longer one of simple inquiry but of horrified understanding;—the gaze of one who heard.

Meantime, Hazen was answering in painful gasps the lawyer's pointed question, "Did you see the face of this body as well as the arm?"

"Did I see—God help me, yes. Just a glimpse, but I knew it. Eyes that my mother had kissed, blind—staring—glassed in awe and unspeakable fright. The mouth, whose every curve I had studied in the old days of perfect affection, drawn into a revolting grin and dripping with unwholesome weeds brought down from the shallows. All strange, yet all familiar—my sister—Georgian—dead—stark—but recognizable. Don't ask me if I saw it. I always see it; it is before me now, the forehead—the chin—the eyes—"

Ransom sprang to his feet, Harper also.

The girl in the doorway had gone white as death, and with outstretched arms and frantic, haggard eyes was striving to ward off the frightful vision conjured up by her brother's words. The movement made by the two men recalled her in an instant to herself, and she drew back—the hesitating, appealing, anxious-eyed girl whom they all knew. But it was too late. Hazen had seen as well as the others, and leaping in frenzy from his chair stood confronting her—a dominant and accusing figure—between the quietly triumphant lawyer and the crushed, almost unconscious Ransom.

CHAPTER XXVII

SHE SPEAKS

Hazen's face was frightful to see; the more so that physical weakness contended with the outsweep of passion, so great and overwhelming in its power and destructive force that to the two onlookers it seemed to spring from deeper sources than ordinary life and death, and have its birth, as well as its culmination, in the unknown and all that is most terrible in the human mind and human experience.

Anitra's eye was spellbound by it. As it dilated upon this vision of unspeakable wrath and almost superhuman denunciation, her own exquisite face filled with a reflected horror, almost equaling his in force and meaning, till the two awed spectators saw in this moment of startled recognition and the up-gathering of two great natures, the oncoming of some hideous climax for which the many strange and contradictory experiences of the last few days had not served to prepare them.

"You hear!"

In these words Hazen loosed out his soul.

The keen cry of the wind running through the house was his only answer.

"You hear!" he repeated, advancing and laying a determined hand upon her arm. "You have made a mock of us with your pretended deafness. What does it mean—Stop! no more play-acting," he fiercely admonished her, as her eyes assumed a look of startled inquiry and wandered away in vague curiosity to the papers scattered over the floor—"we have had enough of that; you cannot deceive us—you cannot deceive me twice. You played at deafness—why? Because Anitra must have some disability to distinguish her from Georgian? Because you are not Anitra? Because you are Georgian after all?"

Georgian!

The word fell like a plummet into the hollow of that great expectancy. Ransom shivered and even Harper's hard cheek changed color. Hazen only stood unmoved, his look, his grasp, the spirit behind that look and grasp, implacable and determined. Their influence was terrible; slowly she succumbed to it against her will and purpose, the will and purpose of a very strong woman. Her eyes rose in a painful and lingering struggle to his face. Then, with a cry her drawn and parched lips could not suppress, she flashed them in agony on Ransom, and this long-suffering man read in them the maddening truth. They were his wife's eyes; the woman before him was indeed Georgian.

"Speak!" rang out the voice of Hazen, as Harper, realizing from Ransom's face what Ransom had just realized from hers, stepped to the door and closed it. "The time is short; I have much, very much to do. For my sake, for the sake of this much-abused man, whom you allowed to marry you, speak out, tell the truth at once. You are Georgian."

"Yes," fell in almost an inaudible whisper from her lips. "I am Georgian." Then as he loosed his grasp from her arm and she was left standing there alone, some instinct of isolation, some realization of the mysterious pit she had dug for herself and possibly for others, in this avowal of her identity, wrought her brain into momentary madness, and flinging up her arms she fell on her knees before Hazen as under the stroke of some unseen thunderbolt.

"You made me say it," she cried. "On your head be the punishment, not on mine nor on his." Then as Hazen drew slowly back, touched in his turn by some emotion to which neither his look nor gesture gave any clew, she rose to her feet, and fixing him with a look of strange defiance, added in milder but no less determined tones: "A tongue unloosed talks long and loud. You have made me give up my secret, but I shall not stop at that. I shall say more; tell all my dreadful history; yours—mine. I will not be thought wicked because I undertook so great a deception. I will not have this good man's opinion of me shaken; not for a minute; what I did, I did for him and he shall know it whatever penalty it may incur. He is my husband—his love to me is priceless, and I will hold it against you—against the Cause—against Heaven—yes, and against Hell."

Here was truth. To Ransom it came like balm and a renewed life. Bounding across the room, he strove to seize her hand and draw her to himself. But Hazen would not have it. His anger, indeterminate before, was concentrated now, and not the white pleading of her face, nor the warning gesture of Ransom, could hold it back.

"Traitress!" he cried, "traitress to me and to the Cause. You thought to escape what is inescapable. Do you know what you have done? You have—" The rest hung in air. A sudden weakness had seized him and he sank faltering back into a chair Harper pushed towards him, still denouncing her, however, with lifted hand and accusing eyes, the image—though no longer a speaking one—of the implacable and determined avenger.

Georgian, shocked into silence, stared at him in a frenzy of complicated emotions to which neither of them as yet had given the key capable of relieving the maddening tension.

"It is the pool; the pool," she finally murmured. "Its waters have beaten out your life." But he calmly shook his head.

"It is not in water to do that," he murmured. "Give me a moment. I've a question to ask. I think a drop of liquor—"

Harper had flask in hand almost before the word had left the other's mouth. The draft revived Hazen; he looked up at Georgian. "I believe you, so do these men believe you. But you were not alone in this plot. Where is Anitra? Where is the deaf and solitary one you dragged from the streets of New York to bolster up your plot? Tell us and tell us quickly. Where is Anitra?"

"Anitra? Do you ask that?" cried Harper, roused to speak for the first time by his boundless amazement and indignation. "You have described the body in the pool—a description which fits either sister, and yet you would make this woman tell us what you have seen with your own eyes."

He might as well not have spoken. Neither he nor she seemed to hear him. Certainly neither heeded.

"Anitra?" she repeated softly and with a strange intonation. "I am Anitra. I am both Georgian and Anitra. There have never been two of us since I came into this house."

CHAPTER XXVIII

FIFTEEN MINUTES

"There have never been but one of us since I came into this house."

Monstrous assertion! or so it seemed to Ransom as the whirl of his thoughts settled and reason resumed its sway. Only one! But he had himself seen two; so had Mrs. Deo and the maids; he could even relate the differences between them on that first night. Yet had he ever seen them together, or even the shadow of one at the same moment he saw the person of the other? No, and with such an actress as she had shown herself to be these last two days, such changes of appearance might be possible, though why she should engage in such a deep, almost incredible plot was a mystery to make the hair rise,—she, the tender, exquisite, the beloved woman of his dreams.

She saw the maddening nature of his confusion and, springing to him, fell on her knees with the imploring cry:

"Patience! Do not try to think—I will tell you. It can all be said in a word. I was bound to this brother of mine, to do his bidding, to follow his fortunes through life, and up to death, by promises and oaths to which those uttered by me at the marriage altar were but toys and empty air. Anitra, or the dream sister my misery took from the dead, was not so bound, so I strove to secure our joy by the seeming death of Georgian and a new life as her twin. You do not understand; you cannot. You have no measure with which to gauge such men as my brother. But it will be given you. There is no hope now. The weakness of a moment has undone us."

Ransom must have heard her, after events proved that he did, but he gave no token of it. The visions that were whirling through his mind still held it engrossed. He saw her, not as she stood before him now, trembling and appealing, but as she had looked to him in the hall that first night, as she had looked to him down by the mill-stream, as she had looked when she told her story as Anitra, and later when she had faced the landlady as Georgian, and the confusion of it all left no room in his conscience for any other impression. But Mr. Harper, though surprised as he had never been before in all his professional career, lost himself in no such abyss. With the freedom which long-delayed insight into the truth gives to a man of his positive nature and training, he left speculation and all endeavor to reconcile events with her declaration, and plunged at once to the obvious question of the moment.

Fixing his keen gaze on Hazen, he observed very quietly, but with an underlying note of sarcasm:

"If this lady is your sister, Georgian Ransom, and there is no Anitra save the fast fading memory of the child commemorated in your family's monument, then your statement as to the body you saw under the ledge was false?"

The answer came deliberately, unaffected both by the manner of the accusation or by the accusation itself.

"Perfectly so," said he, "I saw no body. Perhaps my description would have been less vivid if I had. My intention you know. This woman had deceived me to the point of making me believe that she was indeed Anitra, the twin, and not my millionaire sister, and Georgian's fortune being necessary to her heir, I wished to cut short the law's delay by an apparent identification. I never doubted from the moment this woman faced with such well-played ignorance the mark of great meaning we had placed upon her door, that Georgian was in the river, as you all believed. Why then not give her a positive resting-place, since this would smooth out all difficulties and hasten the very end for which she had apparently sacrificed herself."

If there was any irony in his heart, his tongue did not show it. Indeed his manner betrayed little. Immobility had again replaced all tokens of anger, and immobility which only yielded now and then to a slight contortion more expressive of physical pain than of mental agitation. Yet in Georgian's eyes he had lost none of his formidable qualities, for the dismay with which she followed his words grew as she listened, and reached its height as he added in final explanation:

"The bag I did draw out of the pool, but only because I had taken it down there in my blouse front. Did you think a man could see that or anything else indeed in that maddening swirl of water?"

"But it was Mrs. Ransom's bag," came from Harper in ill-disguised amazement. Even his sang-froid was leaving him before these evidences of a plot so deep as to awaken awe. "Where did you get it? Not from Mrs. Ransom herself? Her own surprise is warranty for that."

"No, I got it from the river, another reason why I credited her drowning. It was fished up from the sand, a little way from the Fall. My man found it; I had sent him there in a vain hope that he might find evidence of the tragedy which others had overlooked. He did, but he told no one but me. You flung the thing too far," he remarked to Georgian. "You should have dropped it nearer the bank. Only such a prodder as my man Ives would ever have discovered it."

Georgian shook her head, impatient at such banalities, in the face of the important matters they had to discuss. "To the point," she cried, "tell these men what will clear me of everything but a wild attempt at freedom."

"I have said what I had to say," returned her brother.

Georgian's head fell. For a moment her courage seemed to fail her.

Mr. Harper rose and locked the door.

"We must have no intruders here," said he, pausing with a certain sense of shock, as he noticed the faint smile, full of some sinister meaning, which for an instant twisted Hazen's lips at these words.

But the delay was but momentary. With an odd sense of haste he rushed at once to the attack.

Stepping in front of Hazen, he observed with force and unmistakable resolution:

"Your devotion to the legatee Auchincloss cannot possibly be explained by any ordinary feeling of obligation. Your sister has mentioned a Cause. Can he by any possibility be the treasurer of that Cause?"

But Hazen was as impervious to direct attack as he had been to a covert one.

"Georgian will tell you," said he. "When a woman looks as she looks now, and is so given over to her own personal longings that she forgets the most serious oaths, the most binding promises, nothing can hold back her speech. She will talk, and since this must be, let her talk now and in my presence. But let it be briefly," he admonished her, "and with discretion. An unnecessary word will weigh heavily in the end. You know in what scales. You shall have just fifteen minutes."

He looked about for a clock, but seeing none drew out his watch from his vest pocket and laid it on the table. Then he settled himself again in his chair, with a look and gesture of imperative command towards Georgian.

Struck with dismay, she hesitated and he had time to add: "I shall not interrupt unless you pass the bounds where narrative ends and disclosure begins." And Harper and Ransom, glancing up at this, wondered at his rigidity and the almost marble-like quiet into which his restless eye and frenzied movements had now subsided.

Georgian seemed to wonder also, for she gave him a long and piercing look before she spoke. But once she had begun her story, she forgot to look anywhere but at the man whose forgiveness she sought and for the restoration of whose sympathy she was unconsciously pleading.

Her first words settled one point which up to this moment had disturbed Ransom greatly.

"You must forget Anitra's story. It was suggested by facts in my own life, but it was not true of me or mine in any of its particulars. Nor must you remember what the world knows, or what my relations say about my life. The open facts tell little of my real history, which from childhood to the day I believed my brother dead was indissolubly bound up in his. Though our fathers were not the same and he has old-world blood in his veins, while I am of full American stock, we loved each other as dearly and shared each other's life as intimately as if the bond between us had been one in blood as it was in taste and habit. This was when we were both young. Later, a change came. Some old papers of his father fell into his hands. A new vision of life,—sympathies quite remote from those which had hitherto engrossed him, led him further and further into strange ways and among strange companions. Ignorant of what it all meant, but more alive than ever to his influence, I blindly followed him, receiving his friends as my friends and subscribing to such of their convictions as they thought wise to express before me. Another year and he and I were living a life apart, owning no individual existence but devoting brain, heart, all we had and all we were, to the advancement and perpetuation of an idea. I have called this idea the Cause. Let that name suffice. I can give you no other."

Pausing, she waited for some look of comprehension from the man she sought to enlighten. But he was yet too dazed to respond to her mute appeal, and she was forced to continue without it. Indicating Hazen with a gesture, she said, with her eyes still fixed on those of her husband:

"You see him now as he came from under the harrow; but in those days—I must speak of you as you were, Alfred—he was a man to draw all eyes and win all hearts. Men loved him, women adored him. Little as he cared for our sex, he had but to speak, for the coldest breast to heave, the most indifferent eye to beam. I felt his power as strong as the rest, only differently. No woman was more his slave than I, but it was a sister's devotion I felt, a devotion capable of being supplanted by another. But I did not know this. I thought him my whole world and let him engross me in his plans and share his passions for subjects I did not even seek to understand.

"I was only seventeen, he twenty-five. It was for him to think, not me. And he did think but to my eternal undoing. The Cause needed a woman's help, a woman's enthusiasm. Without considering my motherless condition, my helplessness, the immaturity of my mind, he drew me day by day into the secret meshes of his great scheme, a scheme which, as I failed to understand till it had absorbed me, meant the unequivocal devotion of my whole life to the exclusion of every other hope or purpose. Favored, he called it, favored to stand for liberty, the advancement of men, the right of every human being to an untrammeled existence. And favored I thought myself, till one awful day when my brother, coming suddenly into my room, found me making plans for an innocent pleasure and told me such things were no longer for me, that a great and immortal duty awaited me, one that had come sooner than he expected, but which my youth, beauty, and spirit eminently fitted me to carry on to triumph.

"I was frightened. For the first time in my memory of him he looked like his Italian father, the man we had all tried to forget. Once while rummaging amongst my mother's treasures I had come across a miniature of Signor Toritti. He was a handsome man but there was something terrible in his eye; something to make the ordinary heart stand still. Alfred's burned with the same meaning at this moment, and as I noted his manner, which was elevated, almost godlike, I realized the difference in our heredity and how natural to him were the sacrifices for which my mind and temper were as naturally unprepared. With difficulty I asked him to explain himself, and it was with terror that I listened when he did. He may have been made to ask, but I was not made to hear such words. He saw my inner rebellion and stopped in mid-harangue. He has never forgiven me the disappointment of that moment. I have never forgiven him for making me sign away my independence, my holdings, and my life to a Cause I did not thoroughly understand."

"Your life?" echoed Ransom, roused to involuntary expression by this word.

"Surely not your life," echoed the lawyer, with the slow credulity of the matter-of-fact man.

"I have said it," she murmured, her head falling on her breast. At which token of weakness, Hazen stirred and took the words from her mouth.

"The organization," said he, "is a secret one and its code is self-sacrifice. To the band of noble men and women, of whose integrity and far-reaching purpose you can judge little from the whinings of a love-sick girl, life and all personal gratifications are as dust in the balance against the preservation and advancement of universal happiness and the great Cause. I thought my sister, young as she was, sufficiently great-minded to comprehend this and sufficiently great-hearted to do the society's bidding with joy at the sacrifice. But I found her lacking, and—" He stopped and almost lost himself again, but roused and cried with sudden fire, "Tell what I did, Georgian."

"You took my duty on yourself," she conceded, but coldly. "That was brotherly; that was noble, if you had not exacted a vow from me in return, destined to lay waste my whole life. Released from this one great duty, I was to hold myself ready to fulfil all others. At the lift of a hand—a finger—I was to leave whatever held me and go after the one who beckoned in the name of the Cause. No circumstances were to be considered; no other human duty or affection. If it were to enter upon a fuller and more adventurous life, well and good; if it were to encounter death and the cessation of all earthly things, that was well too, and a good to be embraced with ardor. Obedience was all, and obedience at a mere signal! I took the oath and then—"

"Yes, then—" emphasized Hazen in wavering but peremptory tones.

"He told me what had led to all this misery. That as yet this compact was between us two, and us two only. That he had considered my youth, and in speaking of me to the Chief had held back my name even while promising my assistance. That he should continue to consider it, by keeping my name in reserve till he had returned from his mission, and if that mission failed, or succeeded too well, and he did not return, I might regard myself as freed from the Cause, unless my enlarging nature led me to attach myself to it of my own free will. That said, he went, and for a year I lived under the dread of his return and all the obligations that return would entail. Then came tidings of his death, tidings for which he may not have been responsible, but which he never contradicted, and I thought myself free—free to enjoy life, and the fortune that had so unexpectedly come to me; free to love and, alas! free to marry. And that is why," she pursued, in all the anguish of a dreadful retrospect, "I recoiled in such horror and hung, a dead weight on your arm, when on turning from the altar where we had just pledged ourselves to mutual love and mutual life, I saw among the faces before me the changed but still recognizable one of my brother, and beheld him make the fatal sign which meant, 'You are wanted. Come at once.'"

"Wretch!" issued from the frenzied lips of the half-maddened bridegroom, as his glance flashed on Hazen. "Had you no mercy? Have you no mercy now, that you should torture her young, credulous soul with these fanciful obligations; obligations which no human being has any right to impose upon another, whatsoever the Cause, holy or unholy, he represents?"

"Mercy? It is the weakness of the easy soul. There is no ease here," he cried, touching his breast with no gentle hand.

"Then you forget my money," suggested Georgian. "Can you expect mercy from a man who sees a million just within his grasp? I know," she acknowledged, as Hazen lifted that same ungentle hand in haughty protest, "that it was not for himself. I do not think Alfred would disturb a fly for his own comfort, but he would wreck a woman's hopes, a good man's happiness for the Cause. He admitted as much to me, and more, in the interview we held that afternoon at the St. Denis. I had to go to him at once, and I had to employ subterfuge in order to do so," she went on in rapid explanation, as she saw her husband's eye refill with doubt under a remembrance of the shame and anguish of that unhappy afternoon. "I had not the courage to leave you openly at the carriage door. Besides, I hoped to work on Alfred's pity in our interview together, or, if not that, to buy my release and return to you a free woman. But the wound which had changed his face for me had changed and made hard his heart. He had other purposes for me than quiet living with a man who could have no real interest in the Cause. The money I inherited, the rare and growing beauty which he declared me to have, were too valuable to the brethren for me to hope for any existence in which their interests were not paramount. I might return to you, subject to the same authoritative beck and call which had put me in my present position, or I might leave you at once and forever. No half measures were possible. Was I, a bride, loving and beloved by my husband, to listen to either of these alternatives? I rebelled, and then the thunderbolt fell.

"I was no longer on probation, no longer subject to his will alone. I was a fully affiliated member. That day my name had been sent to the Chief. This meant obedience on my part or a vengeance I felt it impossible to consider. While I lived I need never hope again for freedom without penalty.

"'While I lived'; the words rang in my ears. I did not need to weigh them; I knew that they were words of truth. There is no power on earth so inescapable as that exercised by a secret society, and this one has a terrible safeguard. None but he who keeps the list knows the members. You, Roger, might be one, and I never suspect it, unless you chose to give me the sign. Knowing this, I realized that my life was not worth the purchase if I sought to cross the will of my own brother. Nor yours, either. It was the last thought which held me. While I dutifully listened, my mind was working out the deception which was to release me, and when I left him it was to take the first step in the complicated plot by which I hoped to recover my lost happiness. And I nearly succeeded. You have seen what I have borne, what difficulties I have faced, what discoveries eluded, but this last, this greatest ordeal, was too much. I could not listen unmoved to a description of my own drowned body. I, who had calculated on all, had not calculated on this. The horror overcame me—I forgot—perhaps because God was weary of my many deceptions!"

CHAPTER XXIX

"THERE IS ONE WAY"

"Have you done?"

Hazen was on his feet and, rigid still, but oscillating from side to side, as though his strength did not suffice to hold him quite erect, was surveying them with eyes sunk so deeply in his head that they looked like dying sparks reanimated for an instant by some passing breath.

The half-fainting woman he addressed did not answer. She was looking up at Ransom for the sympathy and pardon he was as yet too dazed to show.

Hazen made a move. It was that of physical suffering sternly endured.

"Let me speak," he urged. "I have a question to ask. I must ask it now. Who was the woman who came up from New York with you? There were two of you then."

Without turning her head Georgian replied:

"That was Bela, my maid; the same one who personated me on the afternoon of my wedding."

"That accounts for the coarseness of her neck," Hazen explained with a certain grim humor to the lawyer, who had given a slight start of surprise or humiliation. Then quietly to Georgian:

"Was it she who threw the comb and dropped your bag where my man found it?"

"I threw the comb; threw it from my window before I uttered that loud shriek. It did not go very far; but I had to be satisfied with the fact that it lay in the direction of the waterfall. But it was to Bela I entrusted the flinging of the bag. I gave it to her when she left the coach. I had explained to her long before just what a place she would find herself in when she was set down at the foot of the lane; how she was to make her way in the darkness till she came to where there were no more trees, when she was to strike across to the stream, led by the noise of the waterfall. I was very particular in my directions, because I knew the danger she incurred of slipping into the chasm. It was her fear of this and the more than ordinary darkness, I presume, which made her throw the bag hap-hazard. I simply wanted it dropped on the bank above the waterfall."

"I saw the girl," Mr. Harper broke in. "She wore a black skirt like the one you now wear, a black blouse and a red-checked handkerchief knotted about her throat. But the young woman who was seen leaving these parts the next morning had on some kind of a red dress and wore a hat. Bela had thrown away her hat; it was picked up where the coach stopped and afterwards brought here."

"I know. My plans went deep; I foresaw the possibility of her being recognized by her clothes. To guard against this, I had her skirt and blouse made double, the one side black, the other a bright color. She had simply to turn them. The extra hat she carried with her; it was small and easily concealed. Her neckerchief she probably tucked away. I had its mate in my pocket, and when I left my room by the window, as I did the moment after I had locked the two rooms, it was with my hair pulled down and this neckerchief about my shoulders. How did I dare the risk! I wonder now; but it was life, life I was after; life and love; nothing else would have made me so fearless; nothing else would have given me such confidence in myself or lent such speed to my feet, running as I did in the darkness."

"You ran around the house to the lane, and entered it by the turn-stile."

"Yes, and so quickly that I had time to splash myself with mud and lose all my natural characteristics before any one came to find me. It was Anitra they met, panting and disheveled, at the head of the lane; Anitra in appearance, Anitra in heart. I did not act a part; I was Anitra; Anitra as I had conceived her. To me she was and is an active, living personality. Whenever I faced you in her character, I thought with her half-educated mind; felt with her half-disciplined heart. I even shut my ears to sounds; I would not hear; half the time I did not. Nor did I fall back into my old ways when I was alone. From the minute Georgian closed her door upon you for the last time, and I darkened my skin in preparation for a permanent assumption of Anitra's individuality, I became the imaginary twin, in thought, feeling, and action. It was my only safeguard. Alas! had I only gone one step further and made myself really deaf!"

The cry was bitterness itself, but it passed unheeded. Mr. Ransom could not speak and Hazen had other cares in mind.

"Where is this woman Bela now?" he asked.

Georgian was too absorbed or too unwilling, to answer.

He repeated the question, this time with an authority she could not resist. Rising slowly, she faced him for one impressive moment.

"My God!" came from her lips in startled surprise. "How pale you are! Sit down or you will fall."

He shook his head impatiently.

"It's nothing. Answer my question. Where is this Bela now?"

"I don't know. She is beyond my reach—and yours. I told her to lose herself. I think she is clever enough to do so. The money I paid her was worth a few years spent in obscurity."

The spark lighting his eye brightened into baleful flame, but she met it calmly. An indomitable spirit confronted one equally indomitable, and his was the first to succumb. Turning from her, Hazen took out pencil and paper from his pocket, and, crossing to the window with that same peculiar and oscillating motion of which he seemed unconscious, or which he found it impossible to subdue, he wrote a line, folded it, and before even Harper was aware of his purpose threw up the sash and flung it out, uttering a quick, sharp whistle as he did so.

"What's that you're up to?" shouted the lawyer, rushing to the window and peering over the other's shoulder into the open space below, from which a man was just disappearing.

"Am I a prisoner of the police that you should ask me that?" returned Hazen, haughtily.

"No, but you should be," retorted Harper. "I don't like your ways, Hazen. I don't like what you and your sister have said about the Cause and the conscienceless obedience exacted from its members. I don't like any of it; least of all this passing over of poor Bela's name to one whose duty it will possibly be to make trouble for her."

Hazen smiled and moved from the window. No one there had ever seen such a smile before, and the oppression which it brought heightened Georgian's fear to terror.

"Let be!" she cried, lifting her hands towards Harper in inconceivable anxiety. "A quarrel with him will not help you and it may greatly injure me. Alfred, what am I to expect? Something dreadful, I can see. Your face is not the face of one who forgives, or who sees in a gift of money an adequate recompense for a cowardly withdrawal."

"You read rightly," said he. "Your fortune will be accepted by the Chief, but he will never forget the cowardice. What faith can he put in one who prefers her own happiness to the general good? You must prepare for punishment."

"Punishment!" broke scornfully from Harper's lips.

She hushed him with a look before which even he stood aghast.

"You will only waste words," she cried. "If he says punishment, I may expect punishment." And turning back to Ransom, in a burst of longing and passion, she raised her eyes to him again, saying, "You do not forgive because you do not realize my danger. But you will realize it when I am gone."

Ransom, under a sudden releasement of the tension of doubt and awe which had hitherto held him speechless, gave her one wild stare, then caught her to his breast.

She uttered a happy sigh.

"Ah!" she murmured in the soft ecstasy and boundless relief of the moment, "how I have learned to love you during the fears and agonies of this awful week."

"And I you," was the whispered answer. "Too deeply," he impetuously added in louder tones, "to let any harm come to you now."

She smiled; but desperation fought with love in that smile. Gently releasing herself, she cast another glance at Hazen, upon whose gray and distorted countenance there had settled a great gloom, and passionately exclaimed:

"Had law or love been able to interfere with the judgment of our Chief, I should not have been driven into the herculean task of deceiving you and the whole world as to my real identity." Then with slowly drooping head, and the manner of one who has heard his doom pronounced, she hoarsely whispered; "The death-mark was scrawled upon my door last night. This is never done without the consent of the Chief. No one can save me now, not even my own brother."

"False. I scrawled those lines," declared Ransom. "It was a test—"

"Which I commanded you to make," put in Hazen. Then in fainter and less strenuous tones, "She's right. Georgian Ransom is doomed; no one can save her."

"False again!" This time it was Harper who interposed. "I can and will. You forget that I know the name of your Chief. Conspiracy such as you hint at is indictable in this country. I am a lawyer. I shall protect, not only your sister, but her money."

The smile he received in return evinced no ordinary scorn.

"Try it," said he. Then with a laugh so low as to be almost inaudible, yet so full of meaning that even Harper's cheek lost color, he calmly declared: "No one knows the name of our Chief. Auchincloss is a member and a valuable one—the only one whose name Georgian positively knows; but he's but a unit in a thousand. You cannot reach the Head or even the Heart of this great organization through him, and if you did and punished it, the Cause would grow another head and you would be as far from injuring us as you are now. Georgian is right. Not even I can save her now." Then, with a steady look into each of their faces, he smiled again and one and all shuddered. "But the Cause will go on," he cried in tones ringing with enthusiasm. "Mankind will drop its shackles and we, we shall have unriveted one of its chains. It is worth dying for, I, Alfred Hazen, say it."

Slowly he sank back into his chair. The pallor which had astounded all from the first had now become the ghastly mask of a soul whose only token of life glimmered through the orbits of his fast glazing eyes. He breathed, but in great pants. Georgian became alarmed.

"What is it?" she cried, forgetting her own fears and threats in the horror which his appearance excited. "This is something more than exhaustion from the pounding of that murderous eddy. What have you done? Tell me, Alfred, tell me."

For the first time since his entrance into the room a suggestion of sweetness crept into his tone.

"Simply forestalled the verdict of the Chief," said he. "I was under oath to leave the country to-day on no ordinary errand. I failed to keep my word, believing that the interests of the Cause could be better served by what I have here undertaken than by the fulfilment of my primal duty. But we are not allowed the free exercise of our own judgment, else what man could be depended on? With us, neglect means death, no matter what the excuse or the Cause's benefit. I knew this when I made my choice last night. I have been dying ever since, but only actually since I came into this room. When the doctors decided that I had received no mortal hurt in the eddy, I—"

"Alfred!" The sister-heart spoke at last. "Not—not poison!"

"That is what you may call it here," said he, with a return to his old imperious manner, "but later and to the world it will be kindness on your part to name it exhaustion—the effect of my battle with the water. The doctors will reconsider their diagnosis and blame my poor heart. You will have no trouble about it. It is my heart—I feel it failing—failing—"

He was sinking, but suddenly his whole nature flared up. Bounding to his feet, he stood before them, with eyes aflame and a passionate strength in his attitude which held them spellbound.

"What can law, what can selfish greed, what can self-aggrandizement and the most pitiless ambition effect against men who own to such discipline as this? Nothing. The world will go on, you will try your little ways, your petty reforms, your slow-moving legislation and promise of justice to the weak, but the invincible is the ready; ready to act; ready to suffer, ready to die so that God is justified of his children and man lifted into brotherhood and equality. You cannot strive against the unseen and the fearless. The Cause will triumph though all else fails. Georgian, I am sorry—" He was tottering now, but he held them back with a stern gesture, "I don't think I ever knew just what love was. There is one way—only one—"

But from those lips the explanation of this one way never came. As they saw the change in him and rushed to his support, his head fell forward on his breast and all was over.

CHAPTER XXX

NOT YET

They had laid him on the bed and Mr. Harper, in his usual practical way, was hastening to rouse the house, when Georgian stepped before him and laid her hand upon the door.

"Not yet," said she with authority. "He said there was a way—let us find it before we give up our secret and our possible safety. Mr. Harper, have you guessed that way?"

"No, except the usual one of protection through the law which he scouts. I do not believe, Mrs. Ransom, in any other being necessary. Your brother's threats answered a very good purpose while he was alive, but now that he is dead they need not trouble you. I'm not even sure that I believe in the organization. It was mostly in your brother's brain, Mrs. Ransom; there's no such band, or if there is, its powers are not so unlimited as he would make you believe."

She simply pointed to the motionless form and the distorted face which were slowly assuming an expression of great majesty.

"There is my answer," said she. "Men of his strong attributes do not kill themselves from fancy. He knew what he did."

"And you think—"

"That I will not live a week if I pass that door under the name of Georgian Ransom. Mr. Harper, I am sure of it; Roger, I beg you to believe what I say. It may not come here—but it will come. The mark has been set against my name. Death only will obliterate this mark. But the name—that is already a dead one—shall it not stay so?—It is the one way—the way he meant."

"Georgian!"

It was a cry of infinite protest. Such a cry as one might expect from the long-suffering Ransom. It drew her from the door; it brought her to his side. As their eyes and hands met, Harper stepped back to the bedside, and remembering the sensitiveness of the man before him, softly covered his poor face. When he turned back, Mrs. Ransom was slowly shaking her head under her husband's prolonged look and saying softly:

"No, not Georgian, Anitra. Henceforth Anitra, always Anitra. Can you endure the ordeal for the sake of the safety and peace of mind it will bring?"

"I endure it! Can you? Remember the deafness that marks Anitra."

"That can be cured." Her smile turned almost arch. "We will travel; there are great physicians abroad."

"A sister—not a wife?"

"Your wife in time—Ah, it will mean a new courtship and—Anitra is a different woman from Georgian—she has suffered—you will love her better."

"O God! Harper, are we living, awake, sane? Help me at this crisis. I do not know where I am or what this is she really asks."

"She asks the impossible. She asks what you can, perhaps, give, but not what I can. You forget that this deception calls for connivance on my part, and whatever you may think of me or my profession, deception is foreign to my nature and very repugnant to me."

"And you refuse?"

"Mrs. Ransom, I must."

The hope which had held her up, the life which had returned to body and spirit since this prospect of a possible future had dawned upon her, faded from glance and smile.

"Then good-by, Roger, we shall never have those happy days together of which we have often dreamt. I may stay with you a week, a month, a year, but the horror of a great fear will be over us, and never, never can we know joy."

She threw herself into her husband's arms; she clung to him.

"One moment," she cried, "one moment of perfect happiness before the shadow falls. Oh, how I must love you, Roger, to say such words, to think such thoughts, with the body of the brother I loved so deeply once, lying there dead before us, killed by his own hand."

Ransom softly drew her aside where her eyes could not fall upon the bed.

Harper stopped still where he was, the picture of gloom and uncertainty.

"It must be settled now," said Ransom. "As we leave this room, our relations must remain."

"I cannot but think your fears all folly," muttered Harper. "Yet the responsibility you force upon me is terrible. If it were not for that will! How can I present it to the Surrogate when I know the testator is still alive?"

"You need not. I will do that," said Ransom.

"And the property! Given to a man we none of us know. Property that is not legally his."

"I will make it so," cried Georgian with a burst of new and uncontrollable hope as she saw, as she thought, this conscientious lawyer yielding. "There is paper here; draw up a deed of gift. I will sign it and you shall hold it so that whether I live or die, Auchincloss' title to his money shall be absolute. Thus much I wish to do, that Alfred's life should not have been sacrificed for nothing."

"Let me think."

Harper was wavering.

A half-hour later the door of Ransom's room was flung hurriedly open, and loud cries for Mrs. Deo and the office clerk rang through the house. And when they and others came running at the call, it was to find Mr. Ransom and the lawyer hanging over the recumbent figure of the dead Hazen, and the deaf girl Anitra pointing at the group, with wild and inarticulate cries.

Anna Katharine Green – A Concise Bibliography

The Leavenworth Case (1878)
A Strange Disappearance (1880)
The Sword of Damocles: A Story of New York Life (1881)
The Defence of the Bride, and other Poems (1882)
X Y Z: A Detective Story (1883)
Hand and Ring (1883)
The Mill Mystery (1886)

7 to 12: A Detective Story (1887)
Risifi's Daughter, A Drama (1887)
Behind Closed Doors (1888)
Forsaken Inn (1890)
A Matter of Millions (1891)
The Old Stone House and Other Stories (1891)
Cynthia Wakeham's Money (1892)
Marked "Personal" (1893)
Miss Hurd: An Enigma (1894)
The Doctor, His Wife, and the Clock (1895)
Doctor Izard (1895)
That Affair Next Door (1897)
Lost Man's Lane: A Second Episode in the Life of Amelia Butterworth (1898)
Agatha Webb (1899)
The Circular Study (1900)
A Difficult Problem (1900)
One of my Sons (1901)
The Filigree Ball: Being a Full and True Account of the Solution of the Mystery Concerning the Jeffrey-Moore Affair (1903)
The Amethyst Box (1905)
The House in the Mist (1905)
The Millionaire Baby (1905)
The Chief Legatee' (1906)
The Woman in the Alcove (1906)
The Mayor's Wife (1907)
The House of the Whispering Pines (1910)
Three Thousand Dollars (1910)
Initials Only (1911)
Masterpieces of Mystery (1913)
Dark Hollow (1914)
The Golden Slipper, and Other Problems for Violet Strange (1915)
To the Minute; Scarlet and Black: Two Tales of Life's Perplexities (1916)
The Mystery of the Hasty Arrow (1917)
The Step on the Stair (1923)

www.ingramcontent.com/pod-product-compliance
Lightning Source LLC
Chambersburg PA
CBHW071406170626
46811CB00003B/1286